The Barclay Place

The Barclay Place

A RED BADGE NOVEL OF SUSPENSE

Rae Foley

DODD, MEAD & COMPANY
NEW YORK

Library of Congress Cataloging in Publication Data

The Barclay place.

(A Red badge novel of suspense)
I. Title.
PZ3.D426Bar   [PS3554.E56]   813'.5'4   75-29298
ISBN 0-396-07215-1

ONE

The call came on a gray Sunday afternoon in late January, with Gerald Stephens's voice sounding as clear from New York as though he were speaking to me from across Paris.

He asked the usual questions about how I was getting along and expressed what I considered to be undue concern because Florence Manning, with whom I had spent three months in Rome on a relentlessly cultural tour, had returned to New York, leaving me alone and to my own devices. This was a situation I had greatly enjoyed and I had left at once for Paris and a buying spree for a new wardrobe. Florence felt that she had gained all she needed from her head-on collision with the world of art. I don't think we had missed a single canvas or sculpture as we inched our way through the galleries.

For three months I had trodden in Florence's determined wake, helped by her assured indoctrination to admire the right things. What she failed to teach me, because she never discovered it for herself, was that great art has a personal impact, that it performs its miracle for each individual. Florence's incursion into the world of art was an invasion but never a revelation. And, like Florence herself, it was joyless.

1

Her departure, the week before, had been an immense relief. For the first time in my life I found myself following my own drummer and not trailing behind a more dominant personality. "Anxiety," as Kierkegaard pointed out, "is the dizziness of freedom," and at first I felt hesitant, almost timorous on my own. By the end of a week I had the bit in my teeth and was beginning to dare to enjoy myself. I'm not awfully intelligent, but I did realize that there was a lot of life that Florence could never reveal to me, that I would have to find for myself if I had courage enough.

I didn't, of course, attempt to explain all this to Gerald Stephens when he called me from New York. But belatedly it occurred to me that, although international telephone calls were routine for him, as he owned a flourishing import business, they were not usual in his dealings with me. He wrote regularly, every two weeks, inquiring about my welfare, as though it were he, and not my parents, who was responsible for me. Certainly he was more interested.

So I broke in on a comment he was making about the rigors of winter in New York—somehow I never learned the art of beating around the bush—to say, "What's wrong, Gerald? You have some bad news for me, haven't you?"

"I'm afraid I have, my dear," he said soberly, "and I don't quite know how to tell you. That's why I'm so sorry you are alone."

"My father?" I demanded. "Is that it? Something has happened to my father."

"To both of them, Maggie."

"Both?" I was bewildered. "You mean Father and Mother are dead?"

"They were found this morning when Mrs. Williams drove over to collect for the church."

"But how did it happen? A burglar? Did someone kill them?"

"Heavens, no! Don't start imagining horrors, Maggie. They died in their sleep because of a defective gas heater. You may be comforted by one thing. They never knew. It was quite painless. In a way, a consummation devoutly to be wished."

It takes time to absorb so momentous a fact. I tried to pull myself together, to be coherent, to speak clearly to Gerald, who was waiting anxiously, half a world away, hating his painful task.

"I'll take the first plane," I said.

I could hear the desolation in my own voice. And yet it was not grief I felt; it was the realization that just as the chains had fallen off and I was free, with barely time to taste my freedom, I had to go back, to pick up where I had left off, a shadow trailing behind some dominant person, a disappointment to my family, the one who never measured up.

"Unless you really want to come," Gerald said quickly, and I realized that he had always understood, though he had never referred to my position, "it won't be necessary. And I'm being most unselfish about this because I miss you. But if you want to stay on and find yourself, do so. You probably know that your parents donated their bodies to a medical school for research. There will be a simple memorial service in Barclaysville. People there would be outraged if no tribute were paid to a Barclay. Anyhow, your father would have preferred a minimum of fuss."

Yes, he would have preferred that. He had always been shy, a retiring man, shrinking from any contact with the public. It was my mother who would have hated knowing that her death was to be passed over with so little publicity!

"I'll take care of everything here," Gerald went on. "Your father made me your trustee, as you know. I'll see that you get a suitable income, now that you've outgrown an allowance. Let me know if it isn't sufficient. There will be plenty

3

of money, unless, of course, you develop a taste for yachts and star sapphires. We'll work all that out when the estate is settled, and it's not at all complicated. I'll try to sell the twin houses if I can, though I warn you that real estate is in the doldrums now."

"No, don't do that. Sell the houses, I mean. The Browns have rented the twin house for fifteen years and it would be unkind to make them leave. And I don't want to sell our house."

Gerald was surprised. "Somehow I always had the impression that you weren't happy there."

"But Father was. He called it his haven and his refuge. I can't bear to have it fall into alien hands. I suppose you'd better pension off the MacTavishes and put in a caretaker."

The MacTavishes were the couple who had worked for my parents for years—reliable, competent, and kindly.

"A caretaker," Gerald said. "Someone on the premises. It's always better for a house to have someone living in it. We'll leave it to Terry."

Terry, Theresa Tilson, was Gerald's assistant and general factotum. Frankly she scared the life out of me, a grim, drab woman with the humanity of a computer and the efficiency of one. Gerald said he could not get along without her and that she knew as much about the business as he did. I know he paid her a huge salary, which I could imagine her saving scrupulously for her old age, when she'd still be afraid to spend it.

"Thank you, Gerald. Somehow I find I'm always saying that to you."

"My pleasure now and always, Maggie. Leave the worries to me and go out and find yourself. Good luck to you, my dear. Happy pilgrimage. But don't forget to come home. You are very much missed."

Only when his friendly voice, like an outstretched hand,

was gone did I begin to grasp the full meaning of what he had told me. During the previous night my parents had died of gas escaping from a defective heater. That heater had always been a problem and Mother had been demanding an oil furnace for months. It was one of the few wishes she had expressed that Father had not granted at once and without expostulation. He was a gentle man, a man of peace, who hated conflict as he hated the public arena into which Mother had forced him. But on the subject of the gas heater he had been adamant. The house was his refuge, his roots, and nothing must be changed. I suppose some psychologists would call it a kind of substitute womb.

My grandfather had built the twin houses, an eighth of a mile apart, on a hill overlooking the village that had been named for his grandfather. He had given them to his sons when they married, hoping to keep them home. But my uncle's wife had flatly refused to live in a village, so the twin house had been rented ever since; for the last fifteen years by the Browns, a staid couple who took pride in it and maintained it in perfect condition.

Looking back now, I realized that I had never known my parents well. When Father followed his own inclinations, which was seldom, he lived as retired as it is possible to do in the modern world and in a village where he was looked up to as the leading citizen, with constant demands on him that he was not forceful enough to refuse. Now and then he wrote graceful little essays, which appeared in magazines and later in book form. They reaped glowing reviews and practically no money. He rarely spoke of his own work, partly from modesty, partly because Mother openly regarded it as a kind of fiddling while Rome burned.

Mother, metaphorically speaking, was always at the top of the ladder, fighting the blaze, fighting for worthwhile causes. The word worthwhile was constantly on her lips, and neither

5

Father nor I ever lived up to it. True, she had managed by sheer will power to drive him into running for Congress, and there he had proved to be unexpectedly effective, speaking in a decisive voice and making his position clear on every point without double-talk. The stunned but enthusiastic response aroused in a public unused to men who spoke the truth as they saw it, without regard to popularity or expedience, should have provided a pointer for other men, but it is unlikely it had such an effect. In any case, Father never attempted to make other people over in his own image. But as a freshman congressman he made a name for himself where most representatives remain faceless and even nameless to their constituents. There was talk of the governorship, maybe the Senate, even—

Those two years in Washington were the peak of Mother's life. She entertained lavishly, she made worthwhile acquaintances, she cultivated influential people. I believe she had a dream of seeing herself in the White House, becoming known as the First Lady, perhaps even The Woman of the Year.

And then, when he was forced to return home to campaign for the governorship, Father collapsed with a severe heart attack, as though his body had conspired with him against Mother, where his will could not. The doctors told her somewhat grimly that he had a long and useful life ahead if he avoided stress and strain, but the exertion of running for public office, the distasteful business of handshaking and continual speeches and public appearances might easily kill him.

This was a bitter disappointment to Mother, so bitter that the minor disappointment about me did not matter so much when I finished my first year at college without distinguishing myself scholastically or making any worthwhile acquaintances. Her sense of duty continued to drive her as though the Furies were after her, and she never spared herself, as she was prone to point out. But she made life miserable for everyone around her by trying to make them hew to her line. She had many admirers and a few enemies, but somehow she never achieved a truly warm relationship with anyone, even with Father.

In the sitting room of the hotel suite I had taken in Paris, with Gerald's kindly and concerned voice still ringing in my ears, I tried to work myself into the proper emotion. I even tried to cry as the least tribute I could pay to the sudden death of my parents. I genuinely grieved for my father, but he was now, as he had always been, a gentle, remote person who spoke little and with whom, in all my nineteen years, I had never had a single heart-to-heart conversation. He would have shrunk with distaste and dismay from such a personal invasion.

He was fond of me, I think, in a detached, absent-minded way, but only once had he ever intervened between Mother and me. That was when I balked at returning to college, where I had failed miserably to be the kind of success Mother respected, and refused categorically to join some of her committees and plunge into social work. If I could not succeed scholastically, she pointed out, I should at least carry my share of the world's burdens.

Father said gently, "Let her find her own way, Margaret."

And Mother cried out bitterly, the only time I ever knew her to lose her self-control, "You think I'm to blame, don't you? You blame me for Maggie's failure as you blame me for your heart attack."

But for once she heeded Father's advice, perhaps because he so rarely offered any, and she agreed, with only a wry gesture of defeat, to have me accept Florence's invitation to accompany her on a cultural pilgrimage to Rome.

7

II

For the next three years after the sudden death of my parents, I drifted around Europe. I didn't neglect the museums and the "right things," but I explored the mean streets as well as the broad avenues and I learned to talk to people in restaurants and small cafés and to make friends in an easy, casual, undemanding sort of way. Because I had always lived anonymously in Mother's impressive wake, I had never regarded myself as having any personality or attractions of my own. She had been Margaret Barclay, handsome, brilliant, vibrant with an energy that was like an electric charge, and she dominated without effort any room she entered. I might as well have been invisible. No one ever called me Margaret or the more familiar Peggy or romantic Rita. From the beginning I had been Maggie.

As I began meeting all sorts of people, I was so interested in them that I forgot to be shy. Anyhow, I came to realize that my kind of shyness was only an inverted vanity; I'd been more aware of myself and what people would think of me than I had been of them. I learned to enjoy myself frivolously without any thought of meaningful activities and with no sense of guilt whatsoever. I drifted from Madrid to Amsterdam and from Cairo to Stockholm, where I had a brief affair with a sunny-hearted young Swede who made me discover a bubble of laughter I'd been suppressing all these years and whom I left with only a slight pang and no sense of guilt at all. As Edna St. Vincent Millay said: "For if you can't be sorry, Why you might as well be glad."

I had learned a lot from him, that love could be joyous and unhurting and undemanding. During a magic summer cruising the Greek islands in a boat chartered by a group of congenial acquaintances, I thought often of him with gratitude but without regret.

8

Every two weeks I had a letter from Gerald, asking about me, deploring political corruption, and hoping that I was enjoying myself. I was very fond indeed of Gerald Stephens, who was my father's only close friend, though even there I doubt if friendship ever led to an exchange of confidences.

Now and then, during those three years of freedom and personal discovery, I got a letter from a distant cousin, Hazel Barclay, a middle-aged woman whom I regarded as being more than a little off the beam. Hazel represented the triumph of illogic. On the rare occasions when we met, which were as rare as I could make them, she was always deep in some new cult. At one time she studied palmistry, then crystal gazing, then the occult, and finally astrology. She did not discard one for the rest; they seemed to coalesce in her mind without causing her any confusion.

As she delved more and more into the magic she called mysticism, she felt that she was above worldly matters, but she resented the fact that I was comparatively well-to-do and led an easy life while she was secretary to a much-tried man who had been virtually blackmailed by Mother into giving her a job.

During the last few weeks her letters had changed in tone and she began to urge me to return home. That, after all, was where I belonged. And why should I be so trusting where Gerald was concerned? How did I know he was an honest trustee and not pocketing my money?

In her last letter she was more specific. "He just might be the kind of man to take advantage of your inheritance. I've drawn up your horoscope and I feel you should return at once. You can't go on running away from life; you must face reality, no matter how it hurts. Go back to the house you abandoned three years ago and face what it holds for you. To you, I suppose, it seems a house of death, but we will see it

9

through together. Don't try to evade your inheritance. Your stars will see you through."

I had picked up the letter in the lobby of my hotel and had read it, standing at the desk. "The woman is barmy," I said aloud and saw the clerk's startled expression.

Neither Hazel's absurd implications that Gerald was dishonest, nor her melodramatic reference to the "house of death," nor the findings in my horoscope disturbed me for a moment. But perhaps there was more of Mother in me than I thought. It was true that I had been frivoling away my life and not facing reality. I had played long enough. Anyhow, I was becoming weary of living out of suitcases, drifting from one city, one country, to another. It had all been interesting, but it was a restless life. I needed roots and I thought perhaps I would find them where Father had found them, in Barclaysville.

My decision was made before I knew it, certainly before I thought it out consciously. Early next morning I cabled Gerald Stephens:

Coming home on first flight I can get. Please have Terry put house in shape for me.

TWO

It was twilight when the great plane landed as lightly as a bird at John F. Kennedy Airport three days later. During the descent, I had seen the city lighted up, the great soaring buildings, the endless rows of street lights, miles on miles, the bridges spanning the two dark rivers. I had forgotten how beautiful and exciting the city was. I had found nothing more lovely than this and I began to realize that all the time I had been searching for some unknown quantity it had been right at hand, waiting for me. As I stepped off the plane, I discovered that this was where I belonged, that I had come home.

It seemed even more like home when I found Gerald Stephens in the waiting room, a man of average height, slim, with a long narrow face and rimless glasses, who looked more like a college professor than a successful businessman. His hair was grayer than I had remembered, but clipped as short as ever. Gerald was not a man to follow trends. In his unstressed way he was too secure to need to. He adopted neither fashions in hair nor fashions in speech—"the name of the game," "up tight," "finalize," "the thrust of the conversation." The abuse of the English language did not amuse him. He was about my father's age, nearly fifty.

11

When I touched his arm, his face lighted up with surprise and then with welcome. He had never been a demonstrative man, but now he gave me a warm hug and a cool kiss on the cheek.

"Maggie! I'd hardly have recognized you. How smart you've become. And how do you contrive to look younger than you did three years ago?"

"Paris clothes and an expensive hairdresser."

"Did they give you that new confidence in yourself?"

I had forgotten Gerald's aptitude for seeing below the surface, which, at times, could be disconcerting. Without waiting for my reply, he steered me out of the waiting room to the place where suitcases were tumbling down a chute, being grabbed by weary travelers and the few women who are always convinced that their belongings have been left behind. He handed my baggage checks to a stocky man with a bland, guileless face whom I remembered from the past and whom I had always disliked. I almost said feared.

Sam Stokes was an ex-convict whom Gerald had volunteered to rehabilitate. He had been a bank clerk who absconded with some bonds and was traced to a Miami Beach night club in the company of the dubious female who had led to his downfall. He served Gerald in many capacities, one of them as chauffeur.

"Sam made a fool of himself," Gerald said lightly. "Most of us do at one time or another. I remember seeing Clifford Irving, who wrote the Howard Hughes 'biography,' telling a television audience that he believed everyone has in his makeup a touch of larceny. With Sam it was a question of his feeling for a woman being stronger than his integrity. It is past and done now." And for Gerald the subject was closed.

In the great Lincoln, sleek and shining, we moved toward

12

the city, wrapped in luxury and in warmth, with Sam sure and efficient at the wheel. I was so engrossed in absorbing new impressions and noting the changes in the ever-changing city that I did not think about my destination until Gerald said, "I'm taking you home with me, of course. You gave us such short notice that Terry has had no opportunity to check on your house and make sure it is habitable for you. And, by the way, the twin house was rented yesterday, so you won't find yourself entirely isolated if you insist on this demented idea of yours of going up to Barclaysville in the dead of winter."

"The twin house rented! But what happened to the Browns? They've lived there for years."

"They're getting old, and they decided, all of a sudden, to go out to California where their children are. They are tired of cold weather and being shut off from the world during bad storms and having no deliveries of food any more. Anyhow, the roads are passable only about half the time."

I grinned to myself. Gerald was really piling it on. "If things are as bad as all that, I wonder anyone wanted to rent the twin house."

"Oh, he's an unexceptionable tenant," Gerald assured me.

"He's bound to be if Terry accepted him," I said dryly.

"He's an invalid," Gerald explained, "just out of the hospital, seeking peace and quiet and a place in which to recuperate. He has a manservant to look after him, someone to call on if you need assistance." Though Gerald had always made it a practice never to interfere with my plans, he burst out, almost in spite of himself, "But I can't, for the life of me, see why you won't stay in New York, at least for the winter. You'd be much more comfortable, no problems, and Lord knows you'd be welcome. Your favorite room on the third floor is always ready and waiting for you."

13

"But, Gerald, I never meant to impose on you. I expected to go to the Plaza or the Carlyle for the night and then on to Barclaysville in the morning."

"It's no imposition, as you should know. I'm delighted to have you and I can't understand why you've taken it into your head to go back to a place you've never liked."

"I don't know myself. It just struck me, all of a sudden, that I've been frivoling away my life instead of facing reality." This sounded ridiculous when I put it into words.

It sounded that way to Gerald too. "Is Barclaysville more real than Paris?" When I made no reply, he said, "For a moment you sounded like your mother," which was the first time I realized how intensely he had disliked her.

The car turned off Park Avenue South onto the street on Murray Hill where Gerald lived in a delightful old three-story house, which had held out grimly against change and managed to maintain its dignity and individuality in spite of the soaring apartment building on one side and a big, dilapidated old stone mansion on the other, which had been converted into small offices.

The exterior was much as it had been in the days of the last century when ladies in trailing skirts and huge plumed hats had crossed the sidewalk from their barouches, but inside it had been modernized tastefully, without any conflict with the past. Here past and present lived in a harmony of Gerald's creating.

"It's just the same," I said in delight.

"Nothing ever stays the same, Maggie." Gerald checked me momentarily as Sam pulled in at the curb and came around to open the door. "I'd better warn you. Prepare yourself. I have another house guest."

I found myself giggling at his ominous tone. "You make it sound like Dracula."

14

"It's Hazel Barclay."

"Oh, God!"

"Well, she called the other day and asked about you. I'd just had your cable. She's lost her job, poor thing, because the business folded, and she got only a couple of extra weeks' pay, and she has to wait, apparently, for weeks to get unemployment benefits. I don't really know the exact situation. So, of course, I asked her to come here for a few days." As I made no comment, he said, a trifle defensively, "Well, what else could I do, especially when she knew I hoped to keep you here all winter."

I hugged his arm. "Nothing else, being you. Though what possible claim she has on you, barely knowing you! But prepare me; what's her latest fad?"

"She's gone psychic," he said gloomily. "She sees auras. She is sensitive to atmosphere."

I burst out laughing. "Let's go in and face reality together."

As we scurried across the windy sidewalk and up the three steps that led to the door, Gerald said hurriedly, "By the way, I had Sam pick you up a small car because I knew you'd need some transportation of your own. Only a few thousand miles on it and in tiptop condition. It doesn't use much gas. Sam went over it inch by inch and he added some gadgets that might come in handy: some red flares in case of accident, a couple of flashlights, a fire extinguisher, and something called snowshoes that you can push under the wheels if you get stalled in the snow."

He had timed his little speech so that, as he finished, the door opened and the housekeeper, stout and beaming, said, "Good evening, miss. It's nice to have you back."

I shook hands with her. "Good evening, Mrs. Flower. It's nice to be back."

15

As she started toward the stairs, Gerald called after us, "Cocktails at seven and dinner at seven-thirty. I hope the time change doesn't bother you."

We went in procession up the stairs to the third floor where Gerald had set apart one room to be mine because I had once expressed a preference for it. Mrs. Flower trudged ahead, I was in the middle, and Sam plodded behind, bringing all my luggage, as he was still young enough to enjoy making a display of the amount of weight he could carry. As I went up the familiar steps, I thought how typical it was of Gerald to announce his gift of a car at a time when I had no opportunity to thank him.

Mrs. Flower flung open the door, switched on lights, looked around to assure herself that everything was in perfect condition in the bathroom as well as the bedroom. Sam followed, set down the luggage and opened a couple of luggage racks.

When they had gone, I stood looking around me at the familiar room. I had never felt so welcome in my parents' house. And I noticed that something had been added, a rocking chair, as I had once laughingly told Gerald I had a passion for rockers. Gerald never forgot anything that would please me. I thought sometimes how different my life would have been if he had been my father. One thing sure; he would never have married a dominating woman nor a passively yielding one, for that matter. He'd have wanted a real partnership. What a pity he had never found anyone who suited him.

I had barely removed my fur coat and my suit and was standing in my slip when there was a tap at the door. Before I could answer, Hazel came rushing in. She held me off for a moment, her prominent thyroid eyes summing me up. Then she touched her cheek to mine. Her first words were pure Hazel.

16

"What on earth did you pay for that slip? Such gorgeous lace and on something that doesn't even show. Well, it's nice to be able to afford it, but don't you feel guilty living in luxury with all this poverty and unemployment around?" Without waiting for an answer, she plumped herself down in the rocking chair.

Hazel was my father's second cousin, so that our relationship was remote. She was about forty, plump, with the unlined face of the person who has failed to mature, so that she gave an impression of faded youth rather than of ripe middle age, which, paradoxically, made her seem older than her actual years. She had a tendency to peer closely at people because she was nearsighted, but she refused to wear glasses, coyly quoting Dorothy Parker as the reason, though it was unlikely that, glasses or no glasses, anyone had ever made passes at Hazel. When she was assailed by the inevitable headaches, she refused to consult a physician. She put her faith in quacks, and her faith was boundless.

"How are you, Hazel?"

"Well, I've gone to the bottom of the cycle, but I'm coming around again."

I should have been accustomed to Hazel's sibylline comments, but this one stymied me.

"Emotional rhythm, you know," she said, using the simple kind of language suited to my limited intelligence. "We all have our own rhythm. The pendulum swings from high to low. I have learned how to study my emotional reactions so that I can time accurately those periods of unaccountable depression, knowing that the pendulum will swing again from the dark into the light."

There didn't seem to be any adequate answer to that, so I went into the bathroom to wash and re-do my hair, which I preferred to do without Hazel's unwavering scrutiny. I was always a trifle embarrassed by my hair. It was heavy, with

17

a slight wave, an uninteresting brown, but it hung below my hips and was, in its way, spectacular. Because of its weight I had always wanted to cut it, but my father had protested. "Promise me to let it alone," he said. "It's so lovely." So I continued to battle with it, parting it in the middle, brushing it back smoothly on either side, and gathering it into a heavy roll on the back of my neck.

Though I prolonged the operation as long as possible, Hazel was still there when I returned to the bedroom, watching while Carry, Gerald's elderly maid, unpacked a suitcase.

"Don't unpack any more," I told her, after we had greeted each other. "I'm not staying, you know. Just that one bag holds all I'll need tonight. Thank you for helping."

"It's a pleasure to handle such lovely things," Carry said sincerely, without envy. She looked pointedly at Hazel. "I'll help you dress now, or would you rather do it yourself?"

The hint was wasted on Hazel, who rocked back and forth while I put on an afternoon dress of soft apricot silk with long sleeves, because Gerald didn't change for dinner except on formal occasions. Hazel looked at the material. Fingered it. "St. Laurent?"

"Dior."

"And not even an evening dress! It seems wicked!"

"Why on earth?"

"Spending all that money on luxuries when so many people are jobless. I know how it feels. I'm out of a job myself."

"Gerald told me." As Hazel seemed to expect something more, I said lamely, "I'm awfully sorry."

"Did Gerald say anything to you about us staying here, at least for the winter?"

"Us?"

"Oh, I just wondered. We're the only family left now."

I looked forward to a jolly, jolly dinner on my first night home, with Hazel practically oozing indignation and a sense

18

of grievance. As she was never subtle, she had made it apparent that she believed in a "share the wealth" program in which I was to participate. If I could have foreseen that evening, I'd have gone straight to bed with a headache. Not, of course, that it would have made any difference in the long run. It was too late. Two years too late. Nothing now could alter the course of the bullet that had fallen from a decomposing body or the bullet that would be fired into a living head. To say that I was to blame for what happened because of that sudden impulse to come home was absurd. But it's a shadow guilt I'll always carry with me.

II

In Gerald's small bookroom I found him pouring a cocktail for Terry. I hadn't known that she could do anything as human as take a drink. Somehow it seemed more likely that she was oiled, wound up, and set in motion every day like clockwork. She wore thick glasses in heavy black frames and her dark hair looked as though she never had it set. She was a brunette and wore no makeup except for a pale pink lipstick in a thin straight line.

She got up to shake hands with me, and her hand was unexpectedly shapely and soft, with beautifully cared-for nails. She had put on a black lace dress for the occasion, with a high neck and long sleeves. On Terry it looked funereal rather than festive.

She and Hazel exchanged casual good evenings, so I gathered they had met before.

"So you've decided to come back," Terry said abruptly. "I'm sorry about your house, but I've had no opportunity to check on it and I haven't been able to get hold of the caretaker, Prescott. I'm afraid he may be down with influenza. There's a lot of it up there, you know—the virulent kind. Quite a few deaths."

19

There seemed to be a general conspiracy to prevent me from going to Barclaysville, I thought in some amusement. "With so much unemployment I should be able to find someone to look after the place for me," I said.

"Of course, if you really want to go up there," and Terry made this sound unlikely, "I'll get someone to check on the plumbing. That's the essential thing, you know. If Prescott is out of commission and hasn't drained the water, the pipes may have frozen. Well, I'll see what can be done. If you haven't changed your mind in another week—"

"I intend to go up tomorrow," I told her.

"But I didn't bring the house keys! Really, Maggie, I can't be expected to do the impossible."

"If anyone could, it would be Terry," Gerald said, handing me a cocktail.

Hazel refused. "Alcohol dulls the vibrations," she explained, but no one was kind enough to explore the subject and she subsided, looking sulky but, I thought, obstinate.

Gerald turned, smiling, to me. "Surely you aren't going to go rushing off when I've barely seen you. It isn't a matter of life and death, you know."

There was a queer little silence and then Hazel said, "I certainly hope you'll plan to stay right here. But there's one thing sure. I hope I know my duty. If you intend going back to the house where Cousin John and his wife died in that awful way, I'm going with you."

Seeing my appalled expression, Gerald intervened. "Let's drop the matter for tonight." He knew that I could not say bluntly to Hazel that I did not want her, knowing she had been thrust out on the world without any aptitude for dealing with it, and that once she joined forces with me, only a miracle would ever dislodge her.

In spite of Gerald's efforts, and he was a practiced host, that was a dull dinner, with Hazel persisting in holding the

20

field with a summing up of the characters of everyone she knew and a great many public figures she had never encountered. Hazel had the security of knowing she was always right and an irritating little smile for anyone who ventured to disagree with her. Terry remained as silent as a wooden Indian.

It was a relief when, promptly at ten, she took her departure, accepting gratefully Gerald's offer to have Sam drive her home. Hazel yawned and then covered it quickly. She had no intention of leaving Gerald and me together. But here she was outmaneuvered.

"You're tired, Hazel," Gerald said. "Don't try to sit up for Maggie. I want to talk to her. Good night."

Even Hazel had to concede defeat and she went reluctantly up the stairs. Only when her door closed with something of a slam did Gerald permit himself to smile, and even then he was charitable.

"Poor Hazel! Such a dreary woman. Her gullibility is endless, I think. Right now she sees you as her only refuge from the storm. She intends to cling to you and to convince herself that she is doing her duty by you at whatever cost to herself. That kind of self-deception can be very dangerous. I won't permit her to exploit you."

"But she really is up against it, poor thing."

"If necessary I can find a place for her, filing clerk, or a job in the warehouse, something like that. So far I haven't had to drop any of my people and occasionally I take on a few. My business flourishes like the green bay tree. It's curious, isn't it, that a depression tends to make the luxury trades boom. Something positively immoral about it."

I laughed. "That's what Hazel thinks of my wardrobe. Immoral luxury."

"Immoral, perhaps, but very becoming. You've learned how to dress, haven't you? Among other things."

21

I met his eyes. "Among other things," I agreed.

He did not pretend to misunderstand me nor did he condemn me. He merely nodded. "You've grown up—and very nicely, too."

For a moment he sat looking at me over the rim of his brandy glass, a look to which I was not accustomed, and for the first time in the years I had known him, all my life, I felt a stirring of discomfort in his presence.

"There's an alternative to you going back to Barclaysville," he said, and now his eyes were on his glass, tilting it, watching the drops run down the side, as though aware of my discomfort and trying to relieve it. "Why can't you stay here? Stay here permanently, I mean."

As I was speechless, he set down his glass on the polished table and leaned forward. Once more he was looking at me, but this time it was the familiar Gerald I had always been fond of and at home with. "I want you to marry me, Maggie. I think I've been in love with you ever since you were thirteen, a gawky little girl with braces on your teeth, and a flood of beautiful hair hanging down your back. You could make me a very happy man, my dear—happier than you could possibly know, and I'd try very hard to make you a happy woman. I could do it if love were enough, and, of course, if it were reciprocated."

He must have sensed my shock, because he went on talking gently, not speaking of love now, simply of beginning a new life here with him in New York, rather than going back to a house of which I had few happy memories.

Looking at that familiar, kindly face, I found myself unable to speak. I could not say that I had always thought of him as a substitute father. That would hurt too badly. I clutched in my mind for some answer that would satisfy him without hurting.

"I never guessed how you felt. I'm proud—" As he raised

22

his hand in impatient rejection of the platitude, I said, "You see, Gerald, I don't quite know what drove me home. It's as though I had to do it. I can't explain, but I have to go back to that house before I can look into the future at all. Do I sound as rattlebrained as Hazel?"

"Well, not quite," he said judiciously, and I broke into laughter, which eased the strange new tension between us. "But if you feel you've got to do it, by all means get it out of your system. I won't say anything more now. Not now. But I warn you that in a few months, when you've faced your particular bogy, I'm going to ask you again. I've waited a long time for you to grow up, to free yourself, so that any decision you make will be without any compulsion other than your own heart."

THREE

As I might have anticipated, except that I was too bemused by Gerald's unexpected declaration of love and proposal of marriage to think clearly, Hazel followed practically on my footsteps and settled herself in the rocking chair.

"Well, I couldn't imagine what you two had to talk about all this time unless he was reporting on his trusteeship. I should think by now you'd have a right to handle your own money."

Without answering her, I removed my dress, kicked off my shoes, and slipped into a green velvet robe with matching mules.

For a moment Hazel rocked vigorously. Then she said a trifle wistfully, "It's nice here, isn't it, with the servants and nothing to do but enjoy yourself. Still I suppose you're determined not to stay on indefinitely."

"That's what I keep saying," I pointed out.

"Well, if you don't like living in Gerald's house, we could get a nice little apartment here in New York, at least for the winter."

"We?" I turned at bay.

She refused to understand me. "You'll have to admit it

sounds awful: frozen pipes, a neglected house, blocked roads, and influenza." Her stubby fingers turned round and round the bracelet she was wearing, one my mother had given her for Christmas some years ago, the only pretty thing she owned. Why that should make me feel guilty, I don't know; it was the effect Hazel always had on me. Nevertheless I made up my mind that I was not going to succumb to pressure of any kind, even the hardest to resist, that of pity.

And then, in a few words, she managed to strip me of all my dearly won confidence and sense of security.

"I hope I know my duty, Maggie, and I'm not going to let you go off anywhere by yourself. Your horoscope—" She saw my expression. "Oh, I know you are an unbeliever, but someday you will see the light. But right now there's one thing you've got to do, Maggie, and that is to face your inheritance."

I stared at her blankly and then I laughed. "Are you by any chance trying to make me believe that Gerald Stephens is mishandling my estate? Of all the preposterous—"

"I wouldn't put it past him," Hazel said stubbornly. "I get the strangest sensation when I am with him. And you can't tell me there's not something odd in a man of Gerald's apparently unaggressive nature having a prosperous business that brings him in a perfectly indecent income, and in times like these, too!"

Well, I had often wondered about that myself, but then I would never have guessed that my retiring father would become a vigorous congressman.

"You can't type people so easily, Hazel."

She shrugged and gave me a knowing smile that made me itch to slap her. "That isn't what I meant about your inheritance, dear."

"Well, for heaven's sake, don't be so sibylline! What are you talking about?"

"Heredity. Did anyone ever explain to you how your parents died?"

"Of course. Gas escaping from a defective heater. It had been giving trouble for a long time."

"But who turned on the gas without lighting it?"

I sank on the edge of the bed, feeling cold, though the room was warm. "Just what are you trying to tell me, Hazel?"

"That gas was turned on deliberately, Maggie. Your father did it."

"My father! The gentlest, sanest—"

"Yes, *he* was sane. But your mother—you remember that power complex she had? She was the third generation. Both her mother and her grandmother had to be institutionalized."

"That's not possible."

"People weren't so frank about those things then, Maggie. Naturally it was kept quiet. But I think you ought to know. You'll be better able to face reality. All three women developed that—oh, label it megalomania, paranoia, whatever you want to call it, in middle age. Cousin John was devoted to his wife, but he knew that in his frail condition he could not handle the situation as it grew worse and he could not bear to have her institutionalized. Of course, that's why he was so eager to have you out of the country when it happened."

After a long time I said, "I don't believe it." But for the first time in three years I remembered how my mother had cried out bitterly, "You think I'm to blame, don't you? You blame me for Maggie's failure and you blame me for your heart attack."

Hazel got up to touch my cheek with unexpectedly gentle fingers. "I'm sorry, Maggie. Deeply sorry. But somehow we'll work this out together." She stood waiting for me to say something, anything, and she looked genuinely worried.

26

At last I asked, "Does Gerald know?"

"Why, of course," she said in surprise. "That's how I found out."

II

That night I lay staring at the ceiling, watching lights wheel across it as cars went by, listening to the sound of sleet clawing at the window. It isn't true, I told myself over and over. It isn't true. I haven't inherited madness. I'm a perfectly normal woman. A healthy woman. It isn't true. Just some of Hazel's nonsense, like the time she lived for weeks on black molasses and wheat germ.

But Gerald knew, and Gerald had asked me to marry him. And if it was true, if I had inherited a vein of insanity, that explained, better than anything, why he had made his unexpected offer. That was his way of protecting me. He was too long-established a bachelor, too comfortable in his settled way of life, to want to make a drastic change, to marry a girl young enough to be his daughter. And he had confided in Hazel. That was the clinching point. She had not been lying or living in her usual confused fantasy world when she told me that.

Mad. It was a terrible word. Not like Hazel's harmless delusions. Inherited insanity. Inescapable. But there had been no indications of it so far. Or had there? People were said not to know about themselves. "Everyone but thee and me."

It was like having to face the diagnosis of a terminal illness. There was no escape, only a temporary stay of execution. But one thing was clear; grateful as I was to Gerald for the magnificent sacrifice he had been prepared to make, I was not going to marry him for my own protection and the destruction of his peace. And I wasn't, as Hazel had tentatively suggested, going to share a New York apartment with

27

her, under her eternal vigilance, watching for any suspicious symptoms, which would be enough to drive anyone out of his mind.

I was going back to the house where my father had found his roots and his security. A house of death, Hazel had called it. Only there could I find out the truth. Only there could I learn from local records that went back five generations what truth there might be in the allegation that my mother's family carried a strain of insanity. Only there could I learn whether my father had deliberately brought about his wife's death and his own.

When I began to weigh the possibilities, I found my thoughts steadying, regaining their equilibrium. If my grandmother and her mother had been diagnosed as insane, there would be records somewhere.

I watched until the lights circling the ceiling faded and daylight came, gray, with a strange milky texture. It was after nine, as I saw by my bedside traveling clock, a lovely thing with jeweled hands and an enameled face, which Gerald had given me one year for Christmas.

I rang for breakfast and got up to brush my teeth and put on a warm bed jacket. Through the window I caught a glimpse of snow falling like a blanket and in the mirror I saw my face, looking about five years older.

When Carry came up with my tray, she apologized for the delay. "I didn't expect you to be awake so early. Mr. Stephens said you were to rest as long as you liked."

She settled the tray on my lap and propped another pillow behind me. "Mr. Stephens left a note for you," she said when she had removed covers and poured coffee, "and he's awfully sorry he won't see you for dinner because he has an important appointment with some men who are flying to Japan tomorrow, so he can't postpone it."

28

When I had drunk some of the coffee, carefully because it was scalding, and nibbled a bit of crisp bacon—the poached egg and toast and grapefruit had no appeal after a sleepless night—I tore open the envelope addressed in Gerald's neat writing:

> Sorry about dinner tonight, as I hate to miss a minute of your too-brief visit; that is, if it is really to be brief.
>
> In any case, you won't be able to go to Barclaysville today. Traveler's warnings out. The weather is filthy, with practically no visibility, and it would be too dangerous on the roads, icy as they are, in a car to which you are not accustomed. Anyhow, Terry hopes you will postpone your trip to Connecticut for at least a week. She is greatly distressed about not hearing from Prescott. If you insist on going up, she will send you the house keys.
>
> I am enclosing a ticket for the Barylli quartet, which will provide you with better company for the evening than I could be.

The note was signed merely "Gerald."

In a way, it was a relief to have the decision taken out of my hands. My whole body ached with weariness and my eyes felt tight. I was almost glad that the heavy snowstorm made it impossible for me to leave that day. But I didn't, fortunately, need to depend on Terry for house keys. I had carried my own on my keyring for three years, chiefly because it was so hard to take them off and the key ring, also a present from Gerald, was gold.

I saw little of Hazel all day. When I found her in Gerald's

29

bookroom, reading fortunetelling cards spread out on the table, I tiptoed out.

Terry called to say that Gerald would be free for lunch and wanted me to meet him at the Pierre. I was sure she said the Pierre. Anyhow, I told Hazel and Mrs. Flower that I'd be out for lunch and reached the Pierre at one o'clock. I was mildly surprised not to find Gerald waiting for me, because he had an old-fashioned courtesy that made him arrive ahead of time so as not to keep a woman waiting.

When he had not come by one-fifteen, I asked at the desk whether a message had been left for me. At one-thirty I called his office and his secretary said he had called from the Plaza asking about me. I had him paged, realized at once how disturbed he was, explained my stupid mistake, and urged him to go ahead with his lunch, as I knew he had a busy schedule. I'd eat alone and return to the house.

When I got back, I made no comment about my mistake, knowing that Hazel could be depended upon to make the most of it, pleaded a sleepless night, which was true enough, grabbed the first volume my hand reached in the bookroom, and went to my room to lie down. The book proved to be *Antony and Cleopatra*, which never lost its charm for me. Like most of Shakespeare, I found something new with each rereading. But what stopped me cold was the phrase, "the secret house of death."

I shut the book abruptly, as though shutting out the phrase, but it went on beating inexorably in my mind: "The secret house of death."

You'd better get over this, my girl, I told myself grimly. No brooding. No getting frightened. Pull yourself together. Instead, I fell sound asleep and slept until almost six o'clock, to wake up rested, dismissing my morbid fears as the nonsense they were.

For a moment after dinner I thought Hazel was going to

insist on accompanying me to the concert, but there was only one ticket and Hazel's taste was best exemplified by *The Sound of Music,* whose stickily sentimental tunes she sang off-pitch in a tremulous soprano.

For two hours I listened to early Beethoven and some sturdy Brahms and a Verdi quartet, which was not important but charming.

I came out of the overheated concert hall to find the narrow lobby thronged with people waiting in a forlorn hope for taxis. In New York during a bad storm all the taxis seem to go underground. I was accustomed to walking and I had had little exercise for the past few days and my sable coat was light and warm, with a matching fur hood that protected my head and ears from the biting cold.

The distance, after all, was not too far. Because of the cutting edge of the wind, I walked east briskly and then, after I slipped on a hidden piece of ice, more cautiously.

Traffic was slowed, headlights dimmed by snow; the whole world seemed to be wrapped in a soft cotton wool that dimmed sound as well as light, and I felt as though I were completely isolated in the big teeming city.

At Gerald's street I passed the towering commercial building on the corner and the old house that had been converted into offices, deserted at that time of night.

The attack came so suddenly that I neither heard nor saw anything until the arm came around my neck from the back, jerking me off balance, and cruel fingers reached for my throat, fumbled with the collar of my fur coat, ripping it open, deepening their hold until there were strange darting lights before my eyes and then encroaching darkness.

I was dropped so suddenly that I fell on the icy walk with a thud, gasping for breath. Then someone was pulling me up and I began to struggle.

"It's all right, ma'am, I'm a policeman." He shoved a businesslike revolver out of sight into a shoulder holster and helped me to stand. "How badly are you hurt?"

"He choked me."

"Take anything?"

"He didn't try to take my purse." I was still gasping as I tried to fill my tortured lungs with air. "He just went for my throat."

"Could you identify him?"

I shook my head. "I never saw him."

"Are you going far?"

"No, I live right here."

He took my name and address and made a few notes, including the time.

"Shouldn't you have gone after him?" I asked rather indignantly.

"Can't be in two places at once and I didn't know how badly you'd been hurt or even—" He let that drop. But he waited beside me until Mrs. Flower came to open the door cautiously.

"It's me," I called.

She let me in, wearing a heavy bathrobe and felt slippers, her hair in curlers. The policeman drifted away without her noticing him.

"I'm sorry to wake you. I thought Sam would be up."

"That Sam! I don't know where he is. Mr. Stephens gave him the evening off." She looked more closely at me. "What's happened to you, miss?"

"A man mugged me, right outside the house, but a plainclothes policeman saved me." I felt my throat gingerly.

"Your lovely coat is torn!"

"It can be mended," I said wearily. "No harm done."

I went to bed and fell asleep almost as soon as my head

32

touched the pillow. And then the man's arm came around my neck and I tried to find my way to the Plaza through a door marked "The Secret House of Death."

I woke myself and the household by screaming.

FOUR

"Just a nightmare," I assured Gerald and Hazel when I came down to breakfast dressed in a warm sweater and skirt, a scarf wrapped around my throat to conceal the marks left by those cruel thumbs.

Hazel never took her eyes off me all during the meal and Gerald was watching anxiously. "You're really leaving?" he said when I pushed back my chair and announced that I was going to pack so I could make an early start. Because of road conditions and poor visibility, I'd have to drive slowly.

After a look at me Gerald silenced whatever protest he had been about to make. He came to put his hand on my shoulder, pressing it. "I'll have Sam bring the car around. But what about house keys if Prescott is not on duty? Oh, I'll have Terry send them up to you by messenger."

"That won't be necessary. I still have my own."

He turned toward the door, turned back. "Are you sure?"

"Sure," I told him. Impulsively I kissed his cheek. "Don't worry about me, Gerald." As he smiled wryly, I said, "After all, you know I've traveled all over Europe by myself and never come to any harm." I might have added that the only

34

danger I had encountered had been right outside his own house, but I didn't.

It was after he left that Hazel announced that she was going with me and I'd have to wait for her to pack. Seeing her adamant expression, I did not protest. I hated strife and, anyhow, I was no match for Hazel. My one hope was that, if the place was anywhere near as bad as Terry and Gerald claimed, she'd have enough of it in a few days.

She took her time, dawdling, remembering telephone calls she had to make, and a last-minute dental appointment. It was afternoon before we finally got into the little Gremlin Sam had parked at the curb. He had stowed our luggage on the back seat as well as in the trunk, because I had done some heavy shopping on my last visit to Paris.

"Take it slow, miss, and you'll be all right," he said as he closed the door. In the rear-view mirror I saw him watching as I drove away from the house.

Before we had left the Bronx behind, Hazel had already begun to regret her determination to do her duty and save me from myself. The wipers moved rhythmically but still could not clear the windshield. In my haste to get away I had not taken time to study the dashboard, and now I stole quick glances, looking things over whenever I dared take my eyes off the road. The car was warm but the road surface was treacherous, though snowplows had done their best and snow was piled high on either side of the narrowing highway. I drove at fifty and then forty and finally at a cautious thirty because I didn't dare use my brakes. Outside the city, winter closed in on us, the car was shaken as though by a monstrous fist as gusts of wind struck it. Once I went into a skid that nearly sent me smashing into a stalled truck, and Hazel screamed nervously.

"You asked for it," I reminded her.

It was dark by the time I reached the outskirts of Barclaysville, population 2341 at the last census. If the highways had been bad, the village was worse. I remembered where the shopping center was, parked with some difficulty against a bank of dirty snow, and picked my way through a poorly cleared parking lot with Hazel, a silent martyr, at my heels. She didn't like leaving the warm car, but I didn't dare leave the motor running because I had discovered that the tank seemed to be nearly empty. Either there was a gas leak or the efficient Sam had slipped up. It hadn't occurred to me to look at the gas gauge when we started out.

Of all people it would be Mrs. Williams who recognized me when I stood at the meat counter, hoping that Hazel was better-equipped to cook than I was. I ordered a steak and chops and a roast of beef and veal cutlets and a frying chicken, and piled vegetables and basic supplies, such as flour and milk and butter and eggs, in the cart. Heaven knew when we'd be able to get to a market again, and deliveries had long since become a thing of the past.

After looking at my selection, Hazel added cleaning powders and a number of items I had overlooked. Then, gloomily, she selected half a dozen candles. "You never can tell," she said.

A woman with a rigid hairdo and an impressive bosom bulging under her coat turned to look at me. "Miss Barclay! So you've come home—at last!" As she saw my look of nonrecognition, she said kindly, "I am Sarah Williams— Mrs. Williams. I—found them, you know." She added in a voice that reminded me irresistibly of Hazel, it was so filled with doom, "My dear, how brave you are to go back."

My treacherous tongue made me say, "Do you think I am afraid of ghosts?" I was instantly aware that the whole store was silent, listening avidly. After all, in Barclaysville a Barclay was still news.

Mrs. Williams gave me a forgiving smile. "Of course not. The Church, as you know, does not accept the idea of ghosts. These are surely physical phenomena."

"What are?"

"The lights," she told me. "So many people have seen them. And tracks in the snow. Perhaps," she said encouragingly, "it's only tramps."

Hazel moaned.

"Well," Mrs. Williams said, "I hope we'll see you at service Sunday morning. The new rector is a delightful man and your dear mother was so active in the church. It was when I went to make a collection that I—was responsible for their being found. That couple of theirs hadn't even checked on them, though it was after nine in the morning." A scandalous hour, she implied, for people to be lying in bed, with the world's work waiting to be done.

I wanted to ask her about the heater, but it was impossible, not only because of the people listening but because she would distort the question and, if there had been no gossip, stir some up.

When I had wheeled out the cart and hoisted the brown-paper bags into the already crowded back seat, I started back toward the liquor store.

Hazel clutched at my arm. "Don't do that."

"Why not?"

"People will talk."

"Let them talk!"

There were half a dozen people in the liquor store when I put in my order.

"That's quite a load," the clerk said. "Shall I carry it out for you?"

People turned to look and Hazel said, inevitably, "I told you so."

When we got back in the car, night had fallen and I looked

anxiously at the gas gauge, vibrating over the empty sign, trying to remember where there was a filling station. Fortunately I saw the comforting light when we had come to the end of the village where the main road branched right toward the next town and a narrow gravel road branched left, clearly marked DEAD END, and, after a hundred yards or so, made a long steep dip to a narrow bridge, then a sharp right turn, and climbed upward to the spot above the village where the twin houses stood, an eighth of a mile apart for privacy and with a lovely view in summer. It was now late January.

I pulled up at the pump and sounded the horn. After a few moments I sounded it again.

"Damn the man!" I exclaimed in irritation.

"What's wrong?" Hazel quavered. "Is the place closed?"

"No, the attendant is inside, but he's fallen asleep." I got out of the car, feeling the wind cut into my face, and went to open the door. He lay stretched out in a chair, his feet on the desk, his head against a rusty filing case. He was a large young man with a big nose and an arrogant sort of face. No one to tangle with.

"Hi," I said tentatively. When he did not stir, I rapped loudly on the desk.

He opened his eyes, said sleepily, " 'Wake Duncan with thy knocking,' " and then he was wide awake and on his feet, looking rather sheepish.

"I'm sorry I disturbed your rest," I said sarcastically and then I yielded to his disarming grin. "I must admit it's the first time I've ever been greeted by Macbeth."

He laughed, reached for a thick lined coat, pulled on a cap and gloves, and went out to fill the tank. "It's a bad night to be on the road. Going far?"

"Just three more miles, thank God! I'm nearly home. The Barclay place."

He looked at me sharply—a long, scrutinizing look. "I

don't think you should try it tonight. There's no traffic out that way and the house is supposed to be unoccupied, you know. There's a fair motel back in the village. You may not have noticed it."

I was tired of people trying to prevent me from going to my own home. "I can manage."

He cocked an eyebrow at me. He was even taller than I had supposed, with a rangy body, a jutting nose, and an almost insufferable air of self-confidence. I don't mean vanity, exactly; just the impression he gave of a man who felt competent to deal with anything. A garage man with the cultivated accent of Harvard, who quoted Shakespeare while still half asleep.

"What are you doing out here in weather like this?" he asked.

"What are you doing here at any time?" I countered.

He grinned again. He must have been about twenty-eight, and the grin made him seem younger but not boyish. He must have grown up a long time before.

"I'm just another statistic from the depression," he said cheerfully. "Oh, I forgot that we aren't supposed to call it that. One thing a college education taught me was to learn what's essential, and at the moment that's a place to sleep and enough food to sustain life. The garage provides a cot upstairs, cold but better than being out of doors, and I've learned to make a stew out of practically anything."

Considering his bearing, his color, and his general air of being well-nourished, I had my first doubt about him right then and there.

I was beginning to shiver and he said, "You'd better get in the car."

I did so, but when I'd taken the money out of my handbag, I lowered the window. As I handed it to him, I asked, "But why here?"

"I ran out of gas when I got this far on my motorcycle," he said glibly, "and the owner offered me a shelter for pumping gas when he takes time off. Works out fine." He stood back. "Drive carefully, Miss Barclay. After dark it freezes up."

Hazel cut in. "Would you mind closing the window, Maggie? I'm freezing." We had hardly moved away when she said, "I must say, the way you talk to people you've never met in your life, and a guy who pumps gas at that—"

"What's wrong with pumping gas?"

"It looks queer, that's all."

This was shouted over the blare of the radio. In case I have forgotten to mention it, Hazel was one of those people who cannot live without noise around them. She had had the radio on full blast ever since we left New York. It didn't matter whether news, advertising, soap opera, or music filled the air. How much of it registered, I don't know. It was silence she feared.

So when she declared we were being followed, I paid no attention to her. What with the radio and the wind and the sleet and the swish of the wipers, one of which had developed a protesting squeak, she couldn't have heard the last trump. I told her so, but she merely sniffed in an irritating way.

The young man at the garage who quoted Macbeth need not have worried about my making undue haste. As I took the narrow, winding road that led into the country, I had to force my way along an uncleared country road, the car slipping, sidling coquettishly from one side to the other, while I tried to see through the windshield, which, in spite of the blower, was beginning to freeze over. With only the two houses in the next two and a half miles, it was unlikely that this road would be cleared until the very last, which might be a couple of days, unless another snowstorm delayed things still longer.

40

The car turned halfway around and Hazel moaned. Then we came to the section of road I had been dreading, the steep decline that led to a narrow bridge. I put the car into second gear, then into low, and pumped the brake as lightly as I could, crawling at ten miles an hour. But the brake wasn't holding. The car began to gain momentum, rocketing down the icy road. Hazel screamed.

In a desperate attempt to avoid the narrow bridge with its low railing and the turn I could not possibly negotiate on an icy road at this speed, in desperation I steered the nose of the car straight into a snowdrift. It plowed in until the windshield was flat against the snow. With a long sigh of relief I shut off the motor.

"What are we going to do now?" Hazel quavered. "All along I've had the strangest intuition that—"

I pushed my door open with considerable difficulty and squeezed through, inching my way along the side of the car. I fumbled for the lock to the trunk, pulled it up, and dragged out the big red flashing light, which I set up behind the marooned car as a warning, though no one else was apt to be insane enough to come that way that night. Then I groped for the flashlights provided by the efficient Sam and went to pull open Hazel's door wide enough so she could squeeze out.

"What are we going to do?"

"We are going to walk," I told her grimly. "The alternative is to stay here and freeze."

"What about all that food?"

"We can't carry it and it's a cinch that no one is going to steal it tonight. But I'd give a lot for a good stiff drink right now. Come along, Hazel."

With our flashlights picking out icy snow, we slipped and slithered down to the bridge, which we negotiated safely, and started up the hill. Now we were facing directly into the wind

41

so that we had to bend over to walk, one painful step after another. The bitter air cut through my coat and it must have been worse for Hazel, who had only a cloth coat, but she trudged along valiantly enough, not complaining. Once I saw her stop and rub her nose vigorously and realized that mine, too, was numb. My feet soon lost all feeling and even with fur-lined gloves, my fingers were cold.

"Of all the crazy things to do," Hazel began and checked herself abruptly. No doubt about it, Hazel was going to be a comfort.

And then we came to the crest of the hill and saw a house ablaze with light. I'd never seen so lovely a sight in all my life. Terry's tenant was in residence. In spite of growing exhaustion that made each step more difficult, we found that we were hurrying. We stumbled up the steps and I banged on the knocker.

FIVE

From inside I heard someone call, "Philippe! Someone at the door."

"Can't be. It's just the storm," came a fainter voice, so I banged louder.

Footsteps came quickly along the hallway, which was a duplicate of the one in my house, and the door opened on a chain, a woman's action rather than a man's.

"For heaven's sake, let us in. We're freezing!" I shouted.

There was an exclamation and the man called, "It's a woman," and the door opened.

In our haste to get in, Hazel and I jostled against each other, stumbling into the blessed light and warmth, and stood, teeth chattering, shaking with cold, snow from our coats falling on the carpet, our caked shoes making icy tracks.

The man who had admitted us was slim and wiry, with aquiline features and dark hair and eyes. He was attractive in a tough sort of way, the kind who would be typecast as the villain's stooge, especially the kind with a fatal attraction for women. He had a quality of sex appeal you could feel at ten paces. He had a hairline mustache and sideburns. All he needed was jeans and a leather jacket—and a shoulder holster.

He stared at us, blinking in surprise. His opening comment was not encouraging, "How in hell did you get here?"

There was a tapping sound from the living room on the right and a man came out. There could hardly have been a greater contrast, for my first impression had been that Hazel and I would be safer out in the storm. This man was about thirty, slenderly built, badly underweight, with the deep pallor of prolonged illness. He leaned heavily on a crutch. He looked from one to the other and I thought that, if he was anything like the man called Philippe, Hazel and I were going back into the storm.

"For God's sake, Philippe, close the door and take their coats."

At this I protested mutely, holding mine more closely around me.

He smiled then. "You won't need that. There's a big fire in the living room."

Hazel and I went as fast as we could on numb feet toward the magnet of the fire. "Not too close," our unknown host warned us, "until you thaw out a bit."

So we weren't going to be thrust ruthlessly back into the storm, which, I suspected, Philippe would have done unhesitatingly if he had followed his own inclinations. Instead, at a gesture from his employer, he drew up chairs for us.

"I am Donald Gregory. Philippe, don't stand there as though you had never seen a woman before."

This seemed unlikely, as it was apparent that Philippe had seen a great many women and enjoyed the process.

"Make some coffee right away." Mr. Gregory looked at us in concern. "Have you had dinner?"

I shook my head.

"Unfortunately we have just moved in and we have been

44

more or less camping, but at least Philippe can fix you some ham and cheese sandwiches and some cold fried chicken. Is there any soup to heat up?"

Philippe shook his head.

I knew perfectly well that we had no right to impose on a complete stranger, but that night I'd have accepted hot coffee from the devil. I introduced myself and Hazel.

"I am Margaret Barclay and the twin houses belong to me. This is my cousin Hazel Barclay. We are on our way to the other house, but I had to leave our car in a snowbank three-quarters of a mile from here, just beyond the bridge."

"You seem to me to be very enterprising young ladies," Mr. Gregory said mildly. Hazel sniffed and blew her nose, but her teeth were still chattering too much for her to protest.

"It was a crazy thing to do," I admitted, and regretted the words when I saw Hazel's expression, "but I was eager to get here."

Mr. Gregory gave me the swift, questioning look to which I was becoming accustomed. "You are planning to stay there?" He sounded incredulous.

"Why not?"

"But, my dear, the place has been deserted for years, from what Philippe has heard in the village. Heaven knows what shape it is in."

"But Terry—that is, I understood there has been a caretaker there ever since my parents died."

Philippe came in with a tray holding a pot of coffee, cups and saucers, cream and sugar. He set it down and began to pour out the steaming coffee. "Sandwiches coming up," he said with all the polished courtesy of a short-order cook, in sharp contrast to his gracious employer.

"Get some rum for the coffee," the latter suggested. "That will speed the warming-up process."

Even Hazel did not object to the rum. Her vibrations were

45

of another sort, and the cup clattered against her teeth.

"So I am actually your tenant, Miss Barclay," Mr. Gregory said as Philippe appeared with a plate piled gratifyingly high with sandwiches and four pieces of cold fried chicken. We fell on that food like famished wolves, and Mr. Gregory politely pretended to be unaware of our gluttony, a charming host who appeared to be delighted to give hospitality to two women he had never seen in his life and who had burst in on him unceremoniously, practically demanding shelter.

He was seated in a deep chair with his left leg stretched out and the crutch within reach of one thin hand. Once the edge had been taken off my appetite and I began to thaw out, I was able to take stock of him, careful not to let my curiosity be noticeable. He was a relaxed sort of man and a most attractive one. As Hazel said later, in an uncharacteristic burst of enthusiasm, he resembled the French actor, Louis Jourdan, except for a slightly misshapen nose. He had enough charm for a dozen men, but he did not exploit it. When the light of a table lamp fell on his head, I could see traces of deep scars on his scalp. And when I realized that he wore flesh-colored thin surgical gloves, I suspected that they served to conceal scars or deformity of some kind.

Mr. Gregory explained this himself. "I've just left a hospital where I've been having skin grafts as the result of an explosion."

Knowing Hazel, I was terrified for fear she would ask a lot of personal questions in her determination to find out all about the explosion. Fortunately she did not have a chance.

All of a sudden he exclaimed, "Good Lord, you must have frosted your feet. Take your shoes off."

With some difficulty we removed them and observed that our feet were red and swollen and very painful. One thing I was sure of, I'd never get those shoes on my feet again that night.

When we had drunk two cups of scalding coffee, with a jigger of rum in each cup, and devoured the sandwiches and chicken, even Hazel had thawed out. With the immediate problems of food, shelter, and warmth solved—I recalled what the filling station man had said about the essentials—there was the next step to be faced.

"You say you abandoned your car in a snowdrift?" Mr. Gregory said, and I wondered whether he was trying to figure out how to get rid of us.

"Yes, and it can stay there so far as I am concerned. Anyhow, I won't dare drive it again until it has been repaired. The brakes failed on that long hill down to the bridge."

"That was a close shave!" Mr. Gregory exclaimed.

"But what are we going to do?" Hazel wailed. "All our clothes and food and even our handbags are in it."

"Philippe can take care of it in the morning. If he can't do the repairs, and he's an expert mechanic, we'll call a garage."

"Only a wrecker can haul it out of that snowbank," I said.

"But what are we going to do tonight?" Hazel wailed.

"Philippe can get out the car and take you on to your own house," Mr. Gregory said. "No trouble at all. But, so far as we know, the place is unoccupied and there may be no heat, no utilities. I don't like the idea of two women going into that place at night, not knowing what they might encounter. You'd be much wiser to stay here and then go on by daylight. I have two guest bedrooms."

Personally I was delighted to stay. I could see that Hazel was hesitating over two dilemmas: the impropriety of staying in a strange man's house and the possible risks involved. Characteristically she tackled the second one first.

"One room," she said firmly.

I saw Mr. Gregory's lips twitch and caught a laughing glance that asked me to share his amusement.

47

Philippe went upstairs and I heard him at the big linen closet and then in one of the bedrooms. He came down to nod to his employer. "Everything okay."

I felt I owed him some sort of apology, though he had been grudging enough. "I'm afraid we've put you to a great deal of trouble."

He nodded without denying the trouble. "Anything else?"

"Not tonight," Mr. Gregory said. "Thank you, Philippe." He got up with some difficulty as Hazel and I, saying good night, started slowly up the stairs, our feet so painful we could barely put our weight on them. When we had closed the door of the bedroom Philippe had made up for us, I heard the click as Mr. Gregory dialed a number. I drew a long breath of relief. He was having the car taken care of and we were sheltered for the night. It was a wonderful feeling.

As he tap-tapped his way up the stairs, Hazel noisily turned the key in the lock and wedged a chair under the doorknob.

"Oh, for heaven's sake, Hazel," I protested. "After he's been so incredibly kind. What did you expect—mass rape? In his condition he couldn't seduce Lolita."

"Well, there's the other one. A nasty piece of work, if you ask me. I have an idea I've seen him somewhere before."

"Probably in the post office among the pictures marked THIS MAN WANTED," I said as I climbed into bed and pulled the covers over me, reveling in the warmth of the soft blankets. When my grandfather did things, he did them right, and the twin beds were heavenly comfortable.

Hazel was still worrying about Philippe. "He's a disagreeable and impertinent fellow and I can't see why anyone as cultivated and charming as Mr. Gregory puts up with him, except, of course, that it's hard to get reliable help, especially in the country. Unemployment!" She sniffed. "Just too lazy to work, most people, if you ask me."

48

"I didn't," I told her, but I did not remind her that she, too, was unemployed.

II

The next morning I awakened to dazzling light. The storm had spent itself, the air was clear and cold, and the snow, iced over, was a brilliant reflection of reds and greens and yellows and blues, blinding and beautiful. Stark branches of maples had been encased in ice, every tiny twig a perfect thing of dazzling crystal.

There was plenty of hot water and I took a long, leisurely bath and dressed, feeling refreshed, cheerful, and looking forward to the new day. The only sign of past troubles was the deep purple of the marks on my throat, and again I wrapped a scarf around my neck.

Although my feet were still tender, I decided that with enough effort I could squeeze them into my shoes. Hazel still slept, her mouth a little open, snoring gently. As I moved the chair away from the door, she awakened with a start and looked around her in bewilderment.

"It's a gorgeous day and nearly half-past nine. Time we got moving."

There was no one in sight when I went down the stairs, but from the kitchen came the sound of movements and the appetizing smell of frying bacon. It was not Philippe, it was Mr. Gregory, propped on his crutch, who was frying bacon and sliding bread into a toaster. He turned to smile at me.

"Feel better this morning?"

"I could do with a new pair of feet," I admitted. "But otherwise wonderful. You were truly the Good Samaritan, weren't you? Without your kindness and hospitality Hazel and I might have frozen to death."

"I think it is quite possible," he said gravely. "You were about at the end of your rope, weren't you?"

49

By daylight it was easier to see the scars behind his ears and the slightly, very slightly, misshapen nose. This, I thought, was a man who had suffered greatly and had learned, in the process, an almost superhuman control over his feelings. He had banished self-pity and, except for his delightful smile, his face was oddly expressionless, as though he defied anyone to guess at the ordeal through which he had passed. I could only hope that Hazel's vibrations would prevent her from making some infelicitous remark.

In spite of the thin gloves, he turned the bacon deftly, broke eggs into a dish, added a few drops of water to make them fluffy, and beat them lightly with a fork.

"Scrambled all right? It's the only way I know how to fix them. I'm chef this morning because poor Philippe has an abscessed tooth and he has gone in search of a dentist. He won't forget about your car, you know. He'll check on it as soon as he's been fixed up, but there may be a little delay."

"That doesn't matter at all."

Hazel came stumping into the kitchen, following our voices. "Here," she said practically, taking the tongs from Mr. Gregory, "let me do that for you." She proceeded to finish the breakfast with a practiced ease that greatly relieved me, as I have no culinary ability whatsoever. At her insistence, Mr. Gregory sat at the table, leg stretched out, and watched as she turned bacon, drained it on absorbent paper, poured eggs into the pan, stirring them lightly, and removing them from the heat at exactly the right moment.

"There's no fruit," our host said apologetically. "As I told you, we've just moved in."

"I hope sometime we can really prove our gratitude, Mr. Gregory," I said.

"Indeed, yes," Hazel chimed in, and I gathered that her fear of imminent rape had dissolved during the night.

"We're going to be neighbors for a long time, I hope. Can't it be Donald?"

"All right, Donald."

"And you are Margaret?"

"Well, everyone calls me Maggie."

He smiled. "That's settled then."

Hazel insisted on washing up while Donald and I sat at the kitchen table, talking idly.

"You really are going to brave that house?" he asked.

"Why not?"

"Oh, Philippe hears things in the village, you know. Be sure to call on us in case of trouble. I'm not much use in a scrap at present, but Philippe is agile enough for two."

"What trouble?" I asked bluntly.

"Probably none," he assured me in his pleasant voice, "but it's as well to be prepared."

As Hazel and I got into our coats, he said in concern, "Aren't you going to wait for Philippe?"

"There's only an eighth of a mile between the houses," I pointed out. "Anyhow it's a marvelous day."

"But treacherous underfoot," he warned us. "Do be careful." His expression was troubled as we moved cautiously away from the house, our feet breaking through the crust of icy snow with a crunching sound. The glare of the sun on the ice was almost blinding, and the cold cut into our cheeks and brought tears to our eyes, while our painful feet throbbed with every step.

"And we could just as well be at Gerald's house right now, warm and comfortable—and safe." There was a sob in Hazel's throat and I felt sorry for her, but the wind flattened on my mouth the words of empty cheer and they would have done little to relieve Hazel's mood. She was feeling vibrations again, all of them bad.

51

The house, as we approached it, looked deserted, the windows like blind eyes because of the heavy draperies drawn across them, new to me. The snow had not been shoveled away from the steps. It looked as though the efficient Terry had slipped up for once and her caretaker was not on the job.

Hazel clutched at my arm. "Don't go in!" she cried. "Don't go in! It's a house of death!"

"But you told me I ought to come back and face it."

"I know I did, but that was before—"

"Before Gerald told you I had inherited insanity. Well, it's too late now. Here we are."

SIX

The key turned as smoothly in the lock as though I had used it an hour ago and not three years before. I pushed open the door and Hazel and I went in. The house felt empty and when I called out, I knew there would be no response. Nothing but ourselves lived there. The place was dark and cold and there was an odd, unpleasant, pervasive odor.

"The smell of death," Hazel said hysterically.

Shaking off her restraining hand, I went to push open the heavy draperies and let in the sunshine. At once the familiar room and furniture sprang into view. I pressed the light switch, but nothing happened. I turned on the water in the kitchen. Mercifully it had not been drained nor had it frozen, but both taps ran cold.

We stood huddled in our coats against the stale chill in the air, two women whose only transportation was wedged in a snowbank, without heat or light or hot water or food or a change of clothing. Without, I remembered, even our handbags, which had been abandoned with the rest. And neither of us had the faintest idea how to deal with the heater and the electricity or anything else that was so obviously needed.

Unexpectedly Hazel began to cry. "I should have known

better than to let you have your own way."

I had a retort on my lips but smothered it. I felt as lost as she did and this was no time to inform her that she had nothing to say about what I did. And then the telephone rang, making Hazel break off in the middle of a sob. I went quickly to answer it. At least one thing in the house was working. We weren't completely cut off from civilization. Gerald was probably anxious about me, or Terry was going to explain what had happened to her reliable caretaker.

Instead, a strange voice responded to my "Hello" by demanding, "Who are you?"

"Margaret Barclay."

"Sorry. Guess I have the wrong number."

I had hardly moved away when the phone rang again and again I got the same voice. "Say, what is this?" the man demanded. "Giving me the runaround. No answer last night or the night before. Leave us not play games, huh?"

"This is still Margaret Barclay," I said, "and the number you are calling is 354-7111."

"Am I talking to Cincinnati?"

I laughed then. "This is Connecticut."

"My God!" He hung up.

"Well, at least the phone is working," I said cheerfully. "All the laws of nature have not been suspended, and we are still linked, if remotely, to the human race. Maybe Donald will know whom to call about the heater and the electricity."

"Is it that same gas heater?" she quavered. "The one that —you know."

Before I could reply, there was the welcome sound of a car turning into the driveway. I ran to the window with Hazel crowding behind me. It was the little Gremlin. But it was not Philippe who got out from under the wheel, unfolding like a jackknife. It was the man from the filling station.

He saw us at the window and waved cheerfully. I let him

54

in. "Did Philippe arrange for you to bring us the car?"

"Who's he?"

"He works for the man in the twin house, a Mr. Gregory."

"No, I did it myself."

"*You* did it?"

"Well, I got thinking of the two of you trying to get out here over uncleared roads, so I shut up shop, climbed on my trusty Rosinante, and followed you."

"I told you so," Hazel said in a tone of deep satisfaction.

"Then why—" I began.

"It's cold in here," he said. "Haven't you any heat?"

"I should think you could tell that for yourself," Hazel said tartly.

"Where's your furnace?"

"It's a gas heater." I took a flashlight and led the way to the basement. "The electricity is off too, so we have no lights and no way of cooking or heating water. Nothing works but the telephone."

"You've got your troubles," he agreed calmly. "Just as well I came along." He took the flashlight out of my hand and walked ahead, stopping once to sniff. "Smells as though something had died in here."

I shivered. "Don't tell my cousin," I implored him. "She's on the verge of hysterics now."

He looked at the heater, pulled off his heavy gloves, and groped for matches. In a moment I heard a heartening plop as the heater went on. An examination of the fuse box and some muttering and pulling of fuses in and out, and the basement light flashed. He grinned.

"Everything under control now," he said cheerfully. "I'll bring in your stuff."

Without waiting for any response from me, he went out to the car. He must have made half a dozen trips with suitcases, bags of food, the liquor, which he carried tenderly, and our

55

handbags. While Hazel examined hers to make sure her money was intact, he carried up our suitcases and deposited them in our bedrooms.

Out of habit I had taken the room that had always been mine, giving Hazel the other guest room, with a bath between, which we could share. I was not yet ready to occupy the room in which my parents had died. I felt like an intruder there.

Upstairs the unpleasant smell was stronger and the young man sniffed again, his big nose quivering like a trained dog tracking down dope.

"Where's your attic door?" he asked abruptly.

"That one." I started to lead the way, but with a long step he got in front of me. "I'll take care of this." He closed the door behind him and I heard him going upstairs.

He certainly had lordly ways, I thought, divided between gratitude at having my problems taken so deftly out of my hands and annoyance at his air of assurance. He'd never heard the phrase "By your leave." I heard him walk around the attic and stop. At last he called, "Bring up a broom and a dustpan, will you, and then stand back or, better still, go downstairs."

"What is it?"

"A dead rat."

"Oh, God, that's all we needed!"

"Yeah, that's what I thought."

Thankfully, I went downstairs and did not turn around as he passed us, holding the dustpan at arm's length, and trailing a ghastly stench behind him. Hazel, who had unexpectedly practical ideas, hunted through the grocery bags until she found a room spray, which she used lavishly. Then as the house began to lose its chill, she relaxed for the first time.

"We might as well put this food away," she said briskly. "I got some marrow soup bones and I'm going to put them on to boil and then make a good nourishing hot soup for our lunch."

"Thank heaven you can cook!" I exclaimed.

"Oh, little old Hazel has her uses," she said girlishly.

Our rescuer came in and deposited broom and dustpan in a corner. "Washed them off in the snow after I'd buried the corpse. Well, if that's all—"

"You haven't explained how you managed about the car." As he hovered, giving an unconvincing impression of a menial, I exclaimed, "Oh, for heaven's sake, sit down, Mr. —uh—"

"Dale Curtis. Here, let me do that." He took the heavy iron soup kettle Hazel was trying to lift out of a lower cupboard, set it on the stove, and watched with interest while she put the soup bones in it and covered them with water. "Does anything come out of that?"

"Soup stock," Hazel explained. "Thank heavens the stove is working!"

"Never let anyone say the age of chivalry is dead," I declared fervently. "This is twice in twelve hours that a perfectly strange man has come to our rescue in what, believe me, was our hour of need."

"The guy next door?"

"How did you know?"

"Well, I followed you on my motorcycle until you landed in that snowbank, which was mighty fast thinking on your part, Miss Barclay. You'd never have negotiated that turn. Well, I took a look around, saw that the whole motor was buried in icy snow, so there was nothing I could do about it then. So I sort of drifted along, following your flashlights, to make sure you'd be all right. I saw you go to the twin house and I damned near froze to death while you were both getting warm and probably fed." There was a note of mocking grievance in his voice that made me laugh. "But when I saw you both pass a lighted window upstairs, I figured you were safe for the night. Well, I got up early this morning and took out the wrecker. That was quite an ice pack, lady, and it didn't give up your car easily. Anyhow I hauled it back to the shop and went over it. Those brakes were no good."

"Gerald told me his man had gone over the car inch by inch."

"He didn't go over the brakes. For the life of me I don't see how you got as far as you did without having a bad accident."

"Driving at a snail's pace so I wouldn't need to use them."

"At least you can count on them now."

"This is service over and beyond the call of duty, isn't it?"

"Part of the job," he said cryptically.

"But how are you going to get back?"

"Walk. Just three miles."

"But you've done more than enough," Hazel said. "Maggie can drive you back." She seemed to have recovered from her disapproval of what she termed "filling station guys." That was probably his Harvard accent. Somehow it carries its own built-in guarantee of respectability. "I don't know what we would have done without you: the car, the furnace, the electricity, that dead rat. We wouldn't have known how to cope. When you came, I was just about to tell Maggie we were going straight back to New York if we had to go by taxi."

"It was a pleasure. It's tough for two ladies to be all alone out here in winter without a man to take care of them."

I'm no woman's lib advocate, but this is the kind of male chauvinism that usually makes me see red. At the time all I could think of was how deeply I agreed with him.

"I suppose," he suggested, "if you need anything, you can call on the neighbor who took you in last night."

"Yes, but he's an invalid and lame, and I wouldn't trust that man of his as far as I could throw him," Hazel declared. "I'm sure I've seen him somewhere before, but I just can't place him." With her usual inconsequence she went on, "I think I'll bake some popovers. With a big nourishing soup that should be enough for lunch. The meat is frozen, but I'll get out the roast of beef to defrost for dinner."

Dale looked wistful with such obvious intent that I laughed and said, "We owe you that. Will you stay for lunch?"

"Nothing I'd like better." Promptly he removed his heavy coat. "That is, if you'll put me to work."

"You've already made life bearable for us here. When I think of what this house was like half an hour ago, I don't know how to thank you adequately. And that's besides all the trouble you took with the car. By the way, how much—"

"The garage will bill you," he said hastily, and I found myself studying him with more attention than he appeared to relish.

"And on top of all that, you followed us to make sure we were safe and waited outside the other house in the cold."

"A hero, that's what I am," he said cheerfully. "Just the old Galahad coming out. But while I'm here, I'll take a look around and make sure there are no more rats."

Hazel moaned and I said, "I don't understand it. These houses are very well-built. The basements are solid. I can't for the life of me see how a rat got in."

"Just the same—"

"Oh, go ahead. I'm going up to unpack."

While I unpacked suitcases and cursed the shortage of hangers, and made a list of things we'd have to obtain somehow, I could hear Dale making the rounds of the house,

59

room by room, except for the one in which I was busy. He was thorough, if nothing else. I even heard him tapping the walls.

He was obviously a fast man on the job because, when I returned some two hours later, he had overcome all Hazel's resistance. He was sitting at the kitchen table as though he belonged there. He had been peeling potatoes and onions, scraping carrots and celery for the soup, and now he was asking her about her college major, which had been a study of comparative religion.

"I've spent my life in the search for truth," she was saying in her earnest manner when I joined them.

" 'What is truth? said jesting Pilate, and would not stay for an answer,' " Dale quoted. "Wise man, Pilate."

Hazel smiled pityingly, her customary reaction to a statement with which she disagreed, and which, by implication, became absurd.

By this time the kitchen was beautifully warm and fragrant with the appetizing smell of Hazel's soup. Dale looked at me and gave a soundless whistle, but the impertinence was canceled out by his friendly grin.

"Dior," he declared. I had changed to a red wool dress that fitted like a dream.

"Did you major in dressmaking at Harvard?"

"Not so. But I have a sister." A man who had a sister who could afford to be clothed by one of France's great dressmakers and yet had to find shelter in a filling station? There was considerably more to Dale Curtis than met the eye. He had none of the air of apology or defiance or defeat of the man who has run out of luck. When you saw him full face, you were aware of his engaging grin. In profile the face was harder, almost harsh.

Aware that he had blundered, he said hastily, "She married a guy who was really loaded."

60

"Couldn't he give you a job?" Hazel demanded. She was never aware of indelicacy when she blundered into people's private lives.

"In a way he has," Dale said.

Obviously he did not intend to continue the conversation and at that moment Hazel's attention was distracted. "Maggie, what on earth happened to your throat?"

That morning the marks were purple and angry-looking.

"I was mugged night before last on my way home, right outside Gerald's house, as a matter of fact. Fortunately a plainclothes policeman came to the rescue in the nick of time. I'd almost lost consciousness."

Dale's eyes flickered and he looked closely at the bruises. "I guess you were lucky at that," he said in an odd tone. "The guy knew where the pressure points are and he meant business."

"Did he steal anything?" Hazel asked.

"He didn't want anything. Except my life."

"Why on earth didn't you tell anyone?" Hazel demanded. "Honestly, Maggie, that's just like you; doing weird things."

"Mrs. Flower knew, because she let me in and saw that something had happened, but I didn't want Gerald upset. He was worried enough about my coming up here. And the policeman, of course, got my name and address and made a report on it. At least I suppose so." To change the subject, I asked Dale, "Did you find anything when you went through the house?"

"Nary a sign of a rat."

"I wonder how that one got in?"

"I think," Dale said coolly, "it was planted there, just as the heater was turned off and the fuses pulled out. Someone wanted to drive you away—if you ever managed to get here."

"I don't understand what you are talking about."

"I don't know how many coincidences you can swallow,"

61

he said; "a mugging, brakes tampered with, a house made uninhabitable. No sign that anyone has lived here, but the water in the pipes had not frozen. Which is impossible. Something is very wrong."

"I told you so," Hazel said, and this time I had no retort to make.

SEVEN

After a delicious lunch, for Hazel proved to be a superlative cook and her soup was ambrosia, while Dale, much to her delight, devoured five popovers dripping with butter and two big bowls of soup, I said, "We've kept you for hours. I hope this won't jeopardize your job." I said it reluctantly because it had been nice having this big, competent man in the house, which he had made habitable for us, and, anyhow, he was fun to talk to when he wasn't being infuriating.

"It isn't really a job," he said, "and there isn't enough business to justify keeping the place open. The guy lets me stay out of sheer kindness. I expect he'll be closing down any time now. He's old enough to collect social security and he has a couple of sons who send him a bit each month." He smiled at me. "You can see I've been in no hurry to go back: nice house, nice food, nice girls"—Hazel bridled at that— "and it's warm."

For the first time in our lives Hazel and I were as one. We exchanged a long look, filled with a wild surmise, and then I plunged. "Look here, Dale, there are two rooms over the garage where the couple who used to work for my parents lived, and where our missing caretaker has been staying. But he's out of a job as of now, if he ever shows up. The place is furnished. I don't know what shape it is in because I haven't inspected it since we got here, but we could provide plenty of bedding and you've sampled Hazel's cooking—"

"And," Hazel said bluntly, "we need a man around this house. Otherwise, and I tell you straight, Maggie, we are going back to New York."

Certainly there is nothing like a Harvard accent for engendering trust!

"This," Dale declared, "is the kind of break to which I am not accustomed. I accept with wholehearted gratitude." He reached for his coat. "If I may, I'll drive your car back to the garage to pick up my stuff."

"Well," Hazel said dubiously, as we stood at the window watching him drive off, "I guess it will be all right. Anyhow, it will be better—"

"Much better," I agreed. "I guess."

II

The telephone rang and a voice said, "Maggie? Donald Gregory. I'm afraid I have bad news for you. Philippe says there is no trace of your car anywhere along the road to the village."

"Oh, that's all right. The man from the filling station hauled it out of the snowbank with a wrecker, repaired it, and brought it here this morning, along with our luggage, food, and handbags."

"Well, that's a relief! Neither of us could figure out what had happened. How did he know to whom it belonged?"

"We'd stopped at the filling station on our way here, as we were almost out of gas. He advised me not to try to go any farther last night, but I explained I was only going to the Barclay place."

"Oh, I see. We even thought you might have given up and

64

gone back to New York, making some arrangement about the car yourselves."

"Given up? Why?"

"Well, two women in a deserted house. Is everything all right?"

"It wasn't when we got here," I admitted. "I'll never be able to tell you how thankful we are to have been sheltered in your house last night. If we had managed to get here— well, everything was wrong. No heat. No lights. A dead rat in the attic. It was horrible and neither of us knew what to do. But Dale fixed everything for us and now we are warm and comfortable, unpacked and practically settled in."

"That's fine. You're sure you don't need anything? Philippe is at your call, you know."

Remembering Philippe's sullen, resentful demeanor, his "How in hell did you get here?" greeting, I was glad that we did not need to depend on him.

"Thanks, Donald, but it won't be necessary. We've arranged to have Dale stay in the garage apartment. He can handle any difficulty for us."

"*Stay* there?" Donald was shocked and horrified. "But, my God, you don't know the man! You don't realize what you may be letting yourself in for. This is—my dear girl, it won't do. It just won't do. If you want a man around the place, Philippe can sleep there. I never need him at night, just for running the house, cooking, driving the car."

"Don't worry about me, Donald. Everything is going to be fine."

He didn't like the idea. He didn't approve of it. He assured me over and over that I wasn't aware of the risks involved. A strange man out of nowhere who, for all I knew, might have a criminal background or at least criminal tendencies. Why didn't I let him handle it for me? He'd send the fellow packing in short order if I was afraid to do so.

"Honestly, Donald, you are getting all worked up about nothing, and I do hate—" I broke off, conscious of my ungraciousness.

"You hate having other people arrange your life for you. More power to you. May you never regret it. All right, my dear, not another word of protest. But, at least, if you are going to thwart me by ignoring my advice, you'll have to make it up in some way."

"How's that?" I asked suspiciously.

"Come to dinner tonight. I want to compensate for the inadequate way you were fed last night. Philippe can do a good job when he has the proper supplies, and he has them now. He's French, you know, and good cooking is in his blood. You can't refuse."

I responded to that beguiling tone without hesitation. "We'd love it," I assured him. "Seven?"

"Six-thirty if you want a cocktail. And I do. Several, in fact. Philippe doesn't mind the work, but he balks at overtime."

"Like last night?" I laughed. "All right. Six-thirty it is."

When this invitation had been relayed to Hazel, she stood for a moment lost in thought, and I wondered whether her suspicion of Philippe outweighed her admiration for Donald. "I was wondering," she said, "whether I could wear that blue dress. It's the nicest one I have; I bought it out of a bonus check."

"Why not? It's awfully becoming. By the way, Donald wants us to get rid of Dale and have Philippe sleep over the garage at night."

"I'll never consent to have that man around this place," Hazel said firmly. "And I don't mind telling Donald so." She picked up her little transistor radio, now broadcasting one of those dialogues about the superiority of a brand of soap, and went up to inspect her wardrobe.

66

When Dale returned, I believe both Hazel and I drew a secret sigh of relief. After all, we had turned over the car to a strange man, taking him in a kind of blind trust, and Donald had shaken me more than I cared to admit. I had begun to have qualms, wondering whether we would ever see the car again.

He had strapped a motorcycle on the luggage rack on top of the car and he had a struggle lifting it off. He had brought with him an unexpectedly heavy rucksack. I followed him up the stairs to the little apartment over the double garage, carrying linen and blankets and towels and a couple of pillows. The rooms were supposed to be kept comfortable by electric heaters in living room, bedroom, and bath, but they were cold with the chill of rooms that have been long shut up.

Dale flung open a window to clear the stale air, switched on the heaters, tested lights and hot water. Then he saw the load I was carrying and, with an exclamation, took it from me and dumped it on one of the twin beds. The beds, by the way, had been stripped to the mattresses and thick coils of gray dust under them moved slightly as Dale threw the bedding down.

When he had closed the window and upended his rucksack on the second bed, I said, "Dale, do you realize—"

"No one has occupied these rooms in a long, long time. Is that what you mean?"

"Then what became of Prescott?"

"I can tell you one thing. These rooms have been unoccupied, but it looks to me as though your garage has been used. There are fairly fresh oil traces on the cement floor. I noticed them when I drove your car in. In fact, I think both garage slots have been used, at least occasionally."

"A woman I met in the village store said she was surprised I was coming back. She said there had been lights and tracks in the snow. She thought it might be tramps."

"Tramps? Well, it's possible, of course. But if tramps moved into an empty house, why didn't they turn on the heater and make themselves comfortable? Nothing in the whole place was working."

"Except the telephone," I reminded him. I went on to tell him about the man who had made the mistake in dialing and got me when he was calling Cincinnati. And Donald had called me just a few minutes ago.

"He knew the phone was working?" Dale asked sharply.

"He had assumed everything was working. He was about to have a fit because his man Philippe couldn't find any trace of the Gremlin, and he really did throw a fit when he found we had arranged to have you stay here. He was all set to throw you out." I laughed when I saw Dale's face. "Don't worry. Hazel has taken a strong dislike to Philippe and she wouldn't have him on the place when Donald offered to send him over."

"I'm glad to hear it. Just the same, I'd like to know a lot about this Prescott character who seems to have vanished into space."

"Well, Terry assured me he was thoroughly reliable, but she thought he might be down with flu. Apparently there's a particularly virulent epidemic of flu up here."

"Who says so?"

"Terry."

"Who is this Terry?"

"Theresa Tilson. My trustee, Gerald Stephens, assures me that she is the most competent assistant he ever had, practically infallible. He claims that she is incapable of making a mistake. She's the one who hired Prescott."

"She sure as hell slipped up there."

68

"Well, of course, I decided all of a sudden to come home and cabled that I'd be on the first flight I could make and to have the house ready for me. It was unreasonable because I really didn't give Terry any time to look into things herself. Gerald keeps her fairly swamped with work."

Dale, busy making his bed, said over his shoulder, "What made you decide to come home all of a sudden?"

"It's a bit mixed up in my own mind," I admitted. "A combination of little things. Having it made clear to me that I was frivoling away my life and that I had to come home and face myself, face reality."

Dale grunted as he tucked the blankets in neatly. "Did that trustee of yours want you to come up here?"

"He was horrified. He did his best to persuade me to stay in New York." I laughed. "He even went so far as to ask me to marry him."

Dale shook his head. "The lengths to which some men will go."

"Well, of all the beastly—" I laughed and then my laughter faded as I remembered why Gerald had proposed to me. In the stress of driving from New York, landing my car in a snowbank, the night at Donald's, and the series of contretemps of the day, I had forgotten the threat that hung over me like the sword of Damocles.

Dale was aware of my change of mood but he did not comment on it. "Is this trustee the one who gave you the little Gremlin?"

I nodded. "And that's typical of him. He told me about it at a time when I did not have an opportunity to thank him. He's like that."

"And he had his man go over it inch by inch?"

I nodded again. "Sam is another of Gerald's irreplaceable employees. He's efficiency itself, but I've always distrusted him, which is unfair, as after all, he has paid for his crime."

"What crime?" Dale straightened up from his bedmaking and loomed over me, looking about eight feet tall.

I told him about Sam's slip from grace and his prison term. "I'm just prejudiced, that's all. Gerald is so compassionate and understanding he makes me ashamed. I remember he quoted an ex-convict as saying, 'Everyone has a touch of larceny.' "

"Oh, yeah? That belongs to the school of thought that says, 'Everyone does it. Why not me?' Alibi or excuse?"

"Don't misjudge Gerald. He was just trying to understand, to make allowances."

"I must say," Dale commented mildly, as he began to sort out the stuff he had dumped from his rucksack, "this trustee of yours seems to pick some odd characters. I'm judging Terry's efficiency by the state of this house and the vanishing Prescott, and Sam's by the fact that the gas tank hadn't been more than half filled and," he looked at me, his eyes sober, "the brakes had been tampered with, Maggie."

When I made no reply, he went on, "And a mugging took place right outside your trustee's house. No attempt at theft. A deliberate attempt to strangle you. Who knew that you were going to be out that night and what time you were likely to return?"

"But you can't possibly—"

He took me by the shoulders, shaking me lightly, "Listen to me, girl. There's dirty work at the crossroads. Someone didn't want you to come here. That's so obvious that even you should be able to see it. Now who? And why?"

When I made no reply, he said again, "Who could have known you'd be outside the house at that particular time?"

"Gerald," I said sullenly, unaccustomed to being overborne, balking at the idea of pointing a finger at the man I trusted more than anyone in the world and certainly was

70

fondest of. "And Hazel, if you can bring yourself to believe she had anything to do with it."

"I can't. Go on."

"That's all. That's why it's so ridiculous."

"Think, girl!"

"Possibly Terry," I admitted. "She usually buys Gerald's theater tickets and gets restaurant reservations for him and she'd have known I'd be using the concert ticket because Gerald had an important business meeting to attend."

"Do you know what that meeting was and that he actually attended it?"

"Oh, this is ridiculous! If you only knew Gerald—the gentlest, kindest man I ever knew. He is incapable of violence, even if he had an overwhelming reason."

"No one is incapable of violence. And, by the way, what is this important business he is in?"

"He is the owner of a big and successful important firm."

"Oh, he is!" After a moment Dale said, "And when you were mugged, where was the efficient Sam, who never slips up except when it comes to gas and brakes?"

"I don't know. Out for the evening, I guess, because Mrs. Flower, the housekeeper, had to let me in. She didn't know where he had gone. Gerald had given him the evening off."

"And you still don't smell a rat?"

"But why?" I asked, cornered. "What possible reason could there be for preventing me from coming here?"

"And, in case you managed to do it, making the place uninhabitable for two helpless women."

I was too distressed to gag at the word *helpless*. "I don't know."

"And what has become of the mysterious Prescott?"

"Now that I would like to know."

"No sooner said than done. I'll start inquiries in the vil-

71

lage. Everyone there knows the Barclays, big guns up here." Somehow, in his inimitable way, Dale managed to imply that anywhere else Barclays would be practically invisible, but I didn't challenge him about it. Dale went on, "He'd have to get food somewhere and he'd have to cash his pay checks."

"Of course, if he is ill—flu or whatever—he may be in a hospital somewhere."

"He hasn't been living here, Maggie. Use your eyes. And, incidentally, there is no flu in Barclaysville."

After a long time I said, "Then you don't believe there ever was a Prescott."

"I didn't say that, but he's not here now." His voice changed as he saw my expression. "Does it matter so much?"

"Yes, I wanted to talk to him. I thought he might know something terribly important."

I hesitated only a moment and then I told him of my parents being found dead as a result of gas escaping from a defective heater. And then I poured out Hazel's story that the heater had been turned on by my father without lighting the gas.

"I thought if anyone would know the truth about the gas heater it would be Prescott, who took over at once."

Dale was watching me, a curious expression on his face. "And what made you believe your father would do that—kill his wife and himself? From what I've heard, he was quite a guy."

Almost in spite of myself I told him. When I finished, I was shaking and he went into the bedroom, pawed over the stuff on the unmade bed, and came back with a bottle of Scotch, pinchbottle, I noticed, just the thing you would naturally expect in the rucksack of a man out of work. In a cupboard in the little living room, which held an electric plate, a few dishes and glasses and kettles, in case the couple wanted a snack, he found glasses, dusty from lack of use, which he washed and then poured in a little Scotch and added water.

"Drink up. Someone has really been putting you through the hoops, Maggie, and the time has come to stop it."

"It will never stop until I learn the truth about the heater, one way or the other. Did my father deliberately turn it on without lighting the gas? Did my mother inherit madness?"

"You sound like a soap opera," Dale said, casting cold water over my emotional outburst. "Cut it out!"

"How can I until I know the truth?"

"Well, Prescott isn't the only source of information. What about the couple who worked here?"

"Father left them enough to retire on and they went back to Scotland immediately after the memorial service. Gerald wrote me about it at the time."

"Has it occurred to you that if anything had been wrong with those deaths there would have been questions raised, an investigation, and your couple would have had to remain until some verdict was reached?"

"I suppose people never suspected anything being wrong because the heater had been giving trouble for some time."

"And couldn't that have been the simple answer to your tormenting question?"

I shook my head. "Hazel told me about it, about what Father did and why. About my inheritance—my heredity."

"And who told Hazel?"

"Gerald. I suppose that's why he wanted to marry me, to protect me when I became—to protect me. It would be like him, the kind of magnificent gesture he would make. And you can't expect me to shrug off a thing like insanity. Something is wrong."

"That's sure as hell true. Something is wrong. And we're going to clear it up."

"After all," I said, "this isn't your business."

73

"You'd be surprised," he said, and finished his drink. I was taking mine more slowly, knowing that I'd be having cocktails with Donald later on. When he offered me a refill, I explained this to him.

"Well, well, quite the good-neighbor policy. What do you think of your tenant?"

"Charming," I said enthusiastically. "Even Hazel, who doesn't like men—"

"Oh, doesn't she?" he said, grinning.

I ignored this. "She thinks he looks like Louis Jourdan, that perfectly beautiful movie actor."

Dale choked. "Maggie, what is really bugging you?"

"This business of facing reality."

"It's not a bad idea, if you have guts enough." He took away the glasses and rinsed them carefully. "I know a guy who tried running away from reality and he ran straight to hell." Aware of the bitterness in his voice, he said more quietly, "The chief thing is to find out what reality is. If I'm any judge, your friend Hazel's search for truth has led her into the world of magic, fortunetelling, and the thing she calls mysticism. I wouldn't put it past her to have faith in voodoo. She represents the triumph of illogic over simple fact."

There was enough truth in that to keep me silent.

"Now, you've come up against the bogey, the fear that your father killed your mother because she was insane and that you have inherited madness. My dear, you are as sane as any person I've ever encountered. Touchy, hard to handle, not broke to the saddle—yet. But sane. Trust me, that's true. Remember this: there is always an explanation for the magician's tricks, like sawing the lady in half. That's being done right before your eyes and we are going to find out why—and who."

"You're pretty sure of yourself, aren't you?"

"Sure about some things. And what we don't know we can find out. It's just a question of knowing where to look."

"Well, where?" I challenged his arrogance.

"Get in touch with the couple in Scotland as a starter. They were here at the time."

"So were the Browns. They were tenants in the twin house for years and moved only recently to California."

"Then we'll look into your mother's background."

"There's no one on her side of the family alive."

"There are records. And I'll drift around Barclaysville looking innocent and asking questions that seem harmless enough."

He held my coat. "If we don't get back to the house, Hazel will send either for the police or the vice squad."

75

EIGHT

As we were coming down the stairs from the garage apartment, Hazel ran toward us, holding her coat around her, and I heard Dale chuckle. "To use Hazel's immortal words," he whispered, "I told you so."

"Oh, there you are! I've been calling and looking all over. I couldn't imagine—Terry is on the phone and she is practically frantic, not having expected you to come up here when she had the house keys and she had not had time to give Prescott instructions about getting the house in order."

For once Hazel had not exaggerated. The usually controlled Terry was in a dither. "If you'd only given me a little time, I'd have arranged everything. I must say, Maggie, I think you've been most inconsiderate. I couldn't make sense out of Hazel. According to her, Prescott isn't there and the house is in bad shape, uninhabitable, and you were stranded in a snowbank last night."

"So far as we can make out, Terry, Prescott has never been near the place."

"But he must have been!"

"Then he's the invisible man and he's left no trace of his presence."

"Oh, dear! I can't understand it. He had splendid recommendations; I checked them carefully at the time."

"How has he been paid?"

"By check, I suppose; how else?"

"Where did he cash them?"

"My secretary balances your accounts and handles all the details. If there had been any checks outstanding, she'd have called it to my attention. But I'll ask her, of course. I can't tell you how horrified I am. In the morning I'll start hunting for a nice apartment for you on Manhattan. How many rooms would you like?"

"Later perhaps. Not now, Terry. There are some things I must do up here."

"But how can you manage? Hazel says everything is wrong."

"*Was* wrong. No heat, no electricity, a dead rat. Most unpleasant."

"How ghastly! I don't see how you've been able to stand it."

"Well, it strikes me someone intended that I wouldn't stand it; that is, if I ever managed to get here in the first place."

"What does that mean?" Terry sounded at a loss for once in her impeccable life. "You are awfully cryptic, Maggie. Not like yourself at all."

"What I mean is that someone didn't want me to come up here." I told her about the abortive mugging and the brakes that had been tampered with. Only by sheer good luck had we been saved from a serious if not a fatal accident.

"Mugged!" Terry's voice went up nearly an octave. "But Mr. Stephens never said a word to me about it, and he'd certainly have done so if he called the police."

"I didn't tell him. The poor man was in such a dither about my coming up here that I didn't want to worry him any

77

farther. And there was no real damage done. My guardian angel must have been on the job that night because a policeman came to the rescue in what is known as the nick of time. I was practically out."

"Maggie! How horrible. Mugging on Murray Hill. I suppose it's all this unemployment that makes people do anything for money."

"There was no attempt to rob me, Terry. The man tried to kill me." As I heard her gasp, I went on, "And next day the brakes on my car were deliberately tampered with. Two attempts at murder in two days are a lot to swallow, don't you think?"

"Murder!" Terry fought for control and now her voice was again quiet, impersonal. "My dear, aren't you reading too much into two isolated incidents? Almost as though you had a feeling of persecution. After all, who would want to injure you?"

"There's only one person who handled the Gremlin," I told her. "And he'd know that I was out for the evening and when I'd be likely to return. And he had the evening off."

"Sam!" Terry was never hasty. She considered all the implications. "Well, between us, I've never trusted him and I never thought Mr. Stephens should give him a job. But you know how he is; when he trusts anyone, it is absolutely. I realize that we should try to rehabilitate criminals, but just the same—"

"Just the same," I agreed.

"I'll talk to Mr. Stephens about it and urge him to get rid of the man. He won't hesitate if he thinks you are in any danger. He thinks a lot of you, Maggie. Sometimes I wonder if you realize just how much he thinks of you."

"I know, but what can you tell him, Terry? I never saw the man who choked me. I haven't a scrap of proof it was Sam. And I certainly don't want Gerald thinking I have a sense of persecution, as you put it. That would only make matters worse. So please don't tell him."

"Well, of course I don't want to interfere in your affairs, Maggie, but Hazel says the house was in awful condition. Somehow I never thought you'd take Hazel along with you. If you went at all, I thought you'd go alone."

"Then you don't know Hazel," I told her, and for the first time I heard Terry give a laugh of genuine amusement.

"Well, there's that of course. I hope you aren't going to share Mr. Stephens's weakness for lame ducks. It doesn't pay. They're never grateful, you know; never satisfied."

"Actually Hazel is being a big help. She can cook, which is more than I can do."

"Then I wonder why you wanted to go up there at all. How are you managing and what about the car in the snowbank?"

So I told her about ditching the car to prevent having it turn over at the bridge and how her new tenant had sheltered us for the night, and this morning a young man from the filling station, where I'd had to stop for gas because Sam had neglected to have the tank filled, retrieved the car with a wrecker, fixed the brakes, and brought it to me along with our luggage and supplies.

"He got the gas heater going, fixed the electric fuses, and buried the dead rat, so now we're doing very well; the house is warm and we're comfortable, Terry. Really we are. Nothing to worry about."

I was careful to suppress the fact that Dale was going to occupy the servants' quarters over the garage, because she'd go into a tailspin and Gerald would probably appear on the scene loaded for bear and prepared to drive the dangerous fellow out.

When Terry at last reluctantly rang off, I sat remembering those cruel thumbs at my throat. Not robbery. Murder. That plus the brakes. Two different people who did not want me to live, or, at least, didn't want me to stay in this house? Unlikely. So unlikely as to be impossible.

Impulsively I dialed the New York Police Department and told them of the mugging incident, the date and place and time, and asked whether my mugger had been caught. There was considerable delay while the right department was reached and the right file identified. Then an apologetic policeman told me that the man had got away.

"The important thing, ma'am, was to make sure you were all right. According to our files, you had dropped to the ground and our man wasn't sure how badly hurt you were. But we'll get this joker sooner or later."

"I hope you get him before he gets me," I said, and the policeman laughed. He thought I was joking.

II

That afternoon there were more wrong calls. One man said, "I'm off for Cincinnati. All set for the twentieth." Another said, "That you, Cincinnati?" and rang off when I said he had the wrong number.

Dale was in the hall near the telephone. I had already discovered that he was a compulsive tinkerer. He had to fool with everything and usually made a great deal of mess before he achieved the result he wanted. At this point he had dismantled the grandfather clock, with parts strewn all around him, and he was happily oiling everything within reach. I doubted if he'd ever put it together again.

"That's four wrong calls, everyone asking about Cincinnati," I said. "There must be something wrong with the phone or someone else has this number. That's going to be a nuisance if it keeps up."

"Same person or different voices?"

"One of them was unpleasant. He said he hadn't had an answer for two nights and didn't want to play games. I didn't like that at all."

Dale grunted and went on with his job. At length he got up with an air of modest pride and looked at the clock, whose pendulum was moving rhythmically and which suddenly bonged out five o'clock.

"Didn't think I could do it, did you?"

"I wronged you deeply."

He grinned then and went out, only to return in a short time wearing his heavy jacket and thick gloves and carrying a lined helmet in his hand. "I'm off to the village if that's all right with you."

"Good heavens, you're a free agent, you know. But don't you want the car?" I looked at the indoor-outdoor thermometer. "It's down to ten already. You'll freeze on a motorcycle."

"I'm a hardy plant; anyhow, you'll need the car when you go to dinner."

"It's only an eighth of a mile."

"Take the car, Maggie, like a good girl. And tell Hazel not to bother with any dinner for me. I'll get something in the village." He sketched a salute and went out. A little later I heard the roar as the motorcycle went off.

Hazel was still splashing in the tub shared by the two guest bedrooms. Tomorrow I'd move into my parents' room and we could have our own baths. It was absurd to be reluctant to use the room.

I did not change from the red wool dress, remembering that the car would have no time to warm up on the way to Donald's house, but I did find a white silk scarf to cover the thumbmarks, because I did not want to discuss them, and once Hazel got hold of a subject, she worried it like a dog

81

with a bone. She had clearly begun to build a picture in her mind of a combined Jack the Ripper and the Boston Strangler.

She spent a long time over her toilet and finally came out in a pale blue silk dress, a fussy affair that left her plump arms bare with an unattractive display of goose flesh, and wearing my mother's bracelet and a lavish amount of my perfume. Donald Gregory had obviously made a tremendous impression.

When he opened the door for us himself, leaning on his crutch, smiling his welcome, I shared her feeling. He was a delightful man. Within minutes we were talking with the ease of old friends about all the interesting things one stores up because there is no one with whom to share them. While he and I sipped martinis, dry and chilled, Hazel drank cranberry juice and smiled fatuously whenever Donald addressed a remark to her. He couldn't have been nicer about it, and I gave him a high score. He saw through her absurdities to the pathos behind them.

All through dinner, and Philippe proved to be a good cook though a surly waiter, the talk moved easily. I had never met anyone with whom I felt less restraint. Donald seemed to be interested in everything.

After the first moments of awkwardness at the table while we tried hard not to be aware of the thin rubber gloves, wondering about the disfigurement they concealed, we enjoyed ourselves thoroughly. Donald had an infectious laugh and though I knew, under his pleasant manner, he was still greatly upset about our having turned the servants' quarters over to an unknown man, he was too well-bred to bring the subject up again. He even bore with Hazel's unbridled curiosity and her attempts, both covert and open, to learn all about the accident that had left him a crippled invalid. He parried every hint or direct question with unchanged good humor, more amused than annoyed by her persistence. I made no attempt to intervene; nothing could come between Hazel and her determination to learn things.

We were having coffee after dinner, while Philippe washed dishes with an unnecessary amount of clatter to indicate his resentment and sense of ill-usage, when Donald said, "What brought you up here, Maggie? You have city girl written all over you."

"Here we go again," I said in resignation. "It was Hazel. She thinks I ought to face reality and return to my old home where something rather awful happened three years ago."

"You needn't look at me in that reproachful way, Maggie. I certainly wouldn't have suggested it if I'd known how things would be here, or how they were with you. But I do believe we should learn to face reality."

Donald gave Hazel his charming smile. "I don't agree with you. I'm all for dreams. I've had a lot of time, of course, to face reality." He glanced down at the gloved hand, at the crutch on which it rested, at the stiff leg stretched out in front of him. "I've had all the reality I can take. To me one of the most shocking weaknesses of the Communist system is that it's all reality. Children don't read fairy tales. They visit factories. There's no place for the imagination, which is not only man's best refuge but the source of all creativity. We need the dreams, Hazel. They sweeten reality. Since I've been forceably retired from the world of action, the dreams have compensated. I'd rather be a purveyor of dreams than of reality any day."

Hazel struggled with this for a moment. "Well, of course, your health has forced you into a kind of retreat from life, but when you are well again—"

"And you think I will be well again?"

"Let me see your hand," Hazel said. "Perhaps I can tell you."

As she stretched out her own, he drew his back almost with a jerk. I wouldn't have believed, even of Hazel, that anyone could be so thick-skinned.

"Sorry," he said, with a little ripple along his jawline, "you wouldn't like it, you know."

"Oh!" Hazel was belatedly aware of her *gaffe*. "Oh, I'm sorry. I just didn't remember." In a hopeless attempt to retrieve her blunder, she said consolingly, "And it probably isn't as horrible as you think it is." Unable to restrain her curiosity, she asked, "What kind of explosion was it?" When he made no response, she said, faltering a little, "Well, I wondered, of course, because of those scars on your head when the light shines on them."

"For heaven's sake, Hazel!" I exclaimed.

She was checked only for a moment. "Well," she said brightly, "palmistry isn't really a wholly dependable guide. Tomorrow I'll draw up your horoscope. Just give me the date of your birth and, if possible, the exact hour."

Donald laughed then, an infectious laugh that relieved my own tension and prevented me from braining Hazel on the spot. "I'm afraid I can't remember that far back. I was very young at the time, you know. And I'm quite satisfied not to look into the future. Look far enough and there's only one ending. The same ending for us all. Let it come when it may, but I have no desire for a timetable."

To stop her, he turned to me and said casually, "How is your house guest working out? Should I have included him in my invitation to make the numbers even?"

"He's not a house guest," Hazel said. "Maggie gave him the rooms over the garage where Prescott was living."

"Prescott?"

I explained that Prescott was the name of the caretaker who was supposed to have been living on the place for three years but of whom there was no trace.

"That's odd," Donald said idly but without much curiosity.

"Not as odd as the rest of the things that have been going on there," I said grimly. "Someone is trying to drive me out."

"My dear," he began helplessly, and I saw the distress in his handsome face. Aware that I did not brook interference lightly, he said, half amused, "What are you imagining? A sinister plot? A spy ring? Mafia headquarters? Political terrorists?"

"Laugh if you like. But with everything else out of order, with no heat in the house, the water had not frozen in the pipes and the telephone was working. Working in an empty house. And people keep calling and asking for Cincinnati."

He thought that over. "I'll take care of that for you."

"How?"

"I'll call tomorrow and arrange to have your number changed."

"Why didn't I think of that myself?"

"While you're in this forgiving mood, let me ask you one more thing about your new tenant. What do you know about him? Why was he so anxious to work his way into your house?"

The disturbing factor was, when it was brought to my attention, that Dale had done everything he could to provoke that invitation to stay. To my surprise it was Hazel who leaped to Dale's defense, whether for his own sake or because of her aversion for Philippe.

"He's a very superior young man who has had a run of bad luck. He's a Harvard graduate and he has nice manners; I watched him eating lunch and you can tell he was nicely brought up. Soup is always a test, I think."

Donald choked and tried to turn it into a cough.

"And," Hazel concluded triumphantly, "his sister is dressed by Dior."

Donald's expressive eyebrows shot up. "Certainly those are most unusual qualifications for a garage man." He looked up as Philippe came storming into the living room.

"Someone searched the rooms over the garage while I was serving dinner and clearing up. Not a professional job because everything is upside-down, as though he worked in a hurry."

"Well," Donald said slowly. He turned his head and met my eyes.

"It couldn't have been Dale," I assured him. "He took his motorcycle when he went to the village tonight. We'd have heard him come back."

"Of course," he said politely, but he didn't believe me.

NINE

When I drove the car into the garage, Dale's motorcycle was in the other slot. I was glad I'd let Hazel off at the door because I did not feel like facing a barrage of questions, and I was out of answers. When I had locked the garage, I stood back, looking up. The apartment blinds had been drawn but there was a sliver of light in the living room. For a moment I was tempted to call Dale and demand an explanation. One thing I was sure of. In the country, where sounds carry, he could not possibly have driven past Donald's house unheard; he must have pushed the motorcycle.

The only reason I could imagine was that he was the man who had searched Donald's garage apartment. Donald had been quite right, of course. I knew nothing about Dale. I had taken him on trust because he had so miraculously come to the rescue, retrieving the car, fixing the heater and the electricity and getting rid of the dead rat. Miraculously?

Dale had leaped at the chance to stay in the garage apartment. He had, I realized now, made a thorough search of the house when he was presumably checking for traces of rats. He had obviously been interested in the telephone calls for Cincinnati. He had told me bluntly that the mugging, the brakes, the condition of the house meant that someone intended to drive me away.

The story of the unemployed and penniless young man sleeping on a cot in the loft of an unheated village garage became more and more unlikely. I realized now that his heavy lined coat was expensive, as were his fur-lined gloves. His slacks were well-tailored and I recalled that when he had tossed off his sweater, I'd seen the name Abercrombie inside the collar. He needed a handout like an extra head.

When I went down next morning to find Hazel stirring up a muffin mixture and scooping out grapefruit, I still had found no answer to my questions. Again—it was becoming a habit—she took me by surprise. I had expected that she, too, would suspect Dale of having searched Donald's apartment. Instead she looked up, said absently, "Good morning, Maggie," and then went on. "I told you all along I didn't trust that man of Donald's. Not just because he's such a surly beast, but there's something wrong about him. I feel it here," and she touched her forehead. "The way he came dashing in to say the servants' quarters had been searched. You know what? I didn't believe a word of it. Burglars wouldn't break into a place that was occupied and they'd know nothing valuable would be kept in the garage. I think he was trying to draw a red herring across the path."

"Well," I said thoughtfully. "Well, I must admit that's the last thing I'd have expected."

"What is?" Dale asked, as he came in by way of the kitchen door. He sniffed. "Hot rolls? Biscuits?"

"Corn muffins," Hazel told him. "We might as well eat out here. It saves carrying things."

He promptly pulled up a chair. "Had a pleasant evening?"

It was Hazel who told him about Philippe's story of someone searching the garage apartment while he was serving and clearing up after dinner.

"My, my," Dale said.

"I ask you, is it likely that anyone would do a thing like that with the house lighted up and our car outside?" Hazel demanded.

"You wouldn't think so," he agreed.

So I put in my ten cents' worth. "How on earth did you manage to get that motorcycle home so quietly?"

"It's a noisy beast. I pushed it the last part of the way so as not to create a disturbance." He couldn't have looked more guileless. "I put in some legwork while I was in the village, Maggie. I checked on the missing Prescott. We were wrong about him. He was around here for a whole year and well-liked in general. A large, rather stout guy with a kindly face and pleasant ways. Had to leave the police force because he had some kind of kidney ailment and couldn't take the hours or the physical demands on him.

"He was paid by money order, which he cashed regularly every week at the post office. He was known at the market where he bought his food, at the barber's where he had a shave and haircut every Saturday, after which he went to a little tavern down the pike for his week's whoopee—a steak and three glasses of beer. Always three glasses."

Dale referred to some notes. "He always wore blue jeans and a red flannel shirt, winter and summer, and a big cowboy hat in which it was assumed he slept, as he was never seen without it except when in the barber's chair. Well, as I say, he was on the job for a year and then he simply disappeared. No more trips to the post office, no more grocery buying, no more visits to the barbershop or the tavern. After a few weeks the tavernkeeper, who used to talk to him when he came in, got the idea he might be sick or have broken a leg or something and he came out here to look. The Volkswagen had disappeared and so had Prescott. Not a trace of him."

"Does this make any sense to you?" I asked, because I was

growing more and more convinced that Dale was withholding information.

"I have a working theory; I don't have a single scrap of proof."

"Does it have anything to do with this house?"

"Well, yes and no. But there's one thing sure. As long as you are determined to stay here and won't be sidetracked, I doubt if anything else will happen."

"Do you have to be so cryptic?"

He made a helpless gesture. "My dear, I don't know anything definite." To put an end to the conversation, he pushed back his chair. Whatever was wrong with Dale, it did not affect his appetite. He had consumed four muffins, half a grapefruit, and three scrambled eggs, as well as three cups of coffee.

"I'm off to the village."

"Do you expect to learn anything more about Prescott?"

"No, but I want to get all new locks for this place. If anyone should be playing tricks, we might as well be prepared. And there are a few other things—"

"Couldn't Prescott's Volkswagen be traced?"

"Oh, I got the license number, but by this time it's a cinch it's either in a dead-car graveyard or it has a new license."

"Then you think something—happened to Prescott?"

The telephone rang and Hazel went to answer it.

"Today," Dale said quickly, "I'm going to check up on the gas heater. That should set your mind at rest."

Before I could make any comment, he waved his hand and went out. A little later I saw the motorcycle move away from the house, with Dale, like a man from Mars in his helmet and face mask, driving fast.

That morning the telephone rang twice. The first call, which Hazel had taken, was from Cincinnati. The second one was the telephone company saying that my number had been changed to 354–7118. So Donald had wasted no time in arranging it. I called to thank him for that and for a pleasant evening.

"No trouble at all," he said about the telephone. "I hope you won't have any further annoyance. I enjoyed having you dine with me and I hope it can be arranged often. I was afraid Philippe's story about someone ransacking the garage apartment might alarm you unduly and I don't want you driven away, Maggie. Not for a long, long time." There was unexpected warmth in his voice and I found myself smiling, though he could not see me. It is nice to be liked.

"I heard your man roar off a while ago."

"He has some errands in the village," I said vaguely. I was careful not to say that he had been at home when I got back the night before.

That afternoon the man appeared. Hazel saw him from her bedroom window, a slim young fellow wearing a heavy lumberman's jacket, a cap pulled down over his ears, a rifle in his hand.

"Come here, Maggie! Look at that. A man with a gun. You'd better call the police."

I joined her at the window. "Oh, nonsense. He's just a hunter."

"But it isn't deer season and anyhow, hunters wear red jackets and caps so they won't shoot each other."

"Deer isn't the only thing in the woods," I assured her, but, after all, it was my land and it was posted. I got into heavy ski pants, sweater and windbreaker, pulled on a cap

91

and went out, in spite of her shrill protests that I was going to get myself shot.

"Don't be such an idiot, Hazel. You act as though he might be an escaped convict or something. In that case he'd hardly be strolling around so openly. Anyhow this is posted land and I'm going to tell him to get off. I won't have any hunting here."

I went around the garage and made my way through the deep snow behind the house and into the woods that, in summer, help to make Connecticut beautiful and where underbrush usually impedes progress. But the underbrush was gone and the trees widely separated. I made no attempt to approach silently and anyhow it would have been impossible as I had to plow my way noisily through deep, frozen snow.

Without warning I stumbled and fell sprawling over a tree stump that was almost hidden by snow. Evidently it had been dug up at some time, because my weight sent us both rolling in the snow.

The noise attracted the man with the rifle, who was walking slowly through the woods, looking from side to side. He came running to help me to my feet.

"Are you hurt?"

I wiped the snow out of my nose and eyes and cheeks. "I fell over a tree stump. It was just lying there loose." I tried to get up with his help, but I seemed to have landed in a spongy spot and my feet kept sinking. He lifted me out and onto solid ground.

He had a narrow face and observant green eyes and a wide mouth that turned upward at the corners.

"I came out to tell you that you are on posted land. This property belongs to me. I am Margaret Barclay."

"Sorry, I didn't realize I was poaching."

"You should have seen the posted signs. What on earth are you hunting at this time of year?"

He looked sheepish. "Well, actually there's a bounty of ten dollars for every fox we kill. They destroy chickens, you know, and the farmers hate them. In times like these ten dollars looks good to me."

"Have you shot many? I thought foxes were disappearing around here."

"Only four in the past month. Either they've left the country or they are too foxy for me."

While he stood talking, he was prodding idly with the butt of his rifle at the place where my feet had sunk in. He prodded again and again. Then his expression changed.

"Miss Barclay, I suggest you go up to your house."

"Why?"

He prodded again.

"What is it?" I demanded.

"I'm afraid the right question is: Who is it?" He added, his green eyes steady on my face, "Well, thank God, you don't panic. Will you go in and call the state police?" He did not seem so young now. In spite of his politeness it was an order and not a request. "And if you have a shovel—"

Hazel had left her vantage point at the upstairs window and was busy in the kitchen when I made my call to the state police. I didn't want to stir her up until it was inescapable. After all, there might be nothing to upset her.

"This is Margaret Barclay. A young man hunting foxes has just found what he thinks is a body buried in the woods behind my house. He wanted me to call you."

"We're on our way. Tell him not to touch anything and to be careful about making tracks."

"It—it's down quite a way. I fell over a stump and my feet kept sinking in. Whatever it is must have been there at least since before that last heavy snow."

I put down the telephone, found that I was shaking, but I went out to the garage and looked among the assorted garden tools, most of them rusty. I gathered up the shovel, thinking resentfully that Dale ought to be here when I needed him, and started reluctantly into the woods. The young man was on his knees trying to dig through the snow with the butt of his rifle. As I came nearer, he got to his feet and took the shovel from me.

"Thank you. You'd better go back to the house. This won't be pleasant."

As he began to dig, I said sharply, "The state police said not to touch anything."

He looked at me as though about to protest and then said "Okay."

We stood looking down at the brush that covered the shallow mound, which could be seen where the young man's digging had cut into the snow. Neither of us spoke, but I saw the deep lines running from his nose to the corners of his lips. He wasn't so young, after all, and he had a hard-bitten look I hadn't noticed in the beginning.

The state police arrived in a surprisingly short time, roof lights blinking, siren screaming. I plowed back to meet them and show them the way.

"Just what happened?" the older of the troopers asked.

I explained that I had seen a young man with a rifle and had gone out to tell him the land was posted and that I'd fallen over a loose stump and under it the ground was sort of yielding. I gulped.

The two troopers went to join the bounty-hunter, who talked rapidly, gesturing, and the men looked first at the loose stump, kicking it idly to one side, and then they stood looking down. After one of them had taken pictures, the other started to dig. I wanted to go back to the house but I couldn't. I stood watching, not wanting to watch, not able to look away. There was a morbid fascination about it.

A glint of light caught my eye and I saw that someone in

94

Gerald's garage apartment was using binoculars. I couldn't really blame Philippe for being curious after hearing the police siren.

The grave was a shallow one that had been covered with twigs. Apparently the body had been buried in the wintertime when the snow was deep, and it had been covered hastily and without too much attempt at concealment, with the idea that no one was likely to come this way to an unoccupied house, until the body was unrecognizable. The tree stump might have been used as a marker.

I was thoroughly chilled and beginning to shake when one of the men gave an exclamation. They all bent over, brushing away snow and then, as one person, they jerked upright, though they continued to look down. The one with the camera took pictures from several angles. I am thankful to say that I was never asked to look at those pictures.

"What is it?" I asked.

"You shouldn't be here, Miss Barclay," one of the troopers said, aware of my presence for the first time. "Go inside. I'm getting help."

"Please tell me."

"It's a man's body. It's been there a long time. Go back, Miss Barclay. This is no place for a woman."

I went in just as the door was flung open and Hazel started out, struggling into her coat. "Maggie, what is going on? What is that police car doing here? Are they arresting the man with the rifle?"

There was no point in trying to keep the thing a secret. "They've found a dead man buried in the woods," I said bluntly.

"You mean the man with the rifle shot him?"

"No, the victim has been dead for a long time. No, don't go out."

Hazel surprised me. Instead of going into hysterics as she

95

was prone to do over trifles, she took command of the situation. "You're half frozen, Maggie. Go get a hot shower and change your clothes. I'll make some coffee. In fact, I'll make a lot. The troopers will want some too. And I'm glad I got stuff for sandwiches. I'll take care of things. You look half sick. Run along, Maggie."

And I did. I stood under a scalding shower until my body looked like a lobster and I had stopped shaking. I changed to warm dry clothes but I could not keep away from the window. More sirens meant that reinforcements had arrived, a large unmarked car and another police car. Men piled out, some in uniform, some in plain clothes, and plowed through the snow to the little group that stood around the shallow grave which held its unknown victim.

Now they were spreading a canvas on the ground and two men in the grave were lifting—I moved quickly away and ran into the bathroom where I retched until I was exhausted.

Hazel, busy making sandwiches at the kitchen table, looked up and scrutinized my face sharply. "You're not half as tough as you think you are, Maggie. You've had a shock. Go and sit by the fire. And no alcohol. What you need is warmth. I'll have coffee for you in a few minutes."

After the steaming coffee I began to feel better. I had only a hazy idea of what was going on, as I kept away from the window. There seemed to be a lot of coming and going, but it was orderly and without the shouting and confusion of television plays. The men spoke in low tones and made a minimum of fuss.

At length we heard feet shuffling and, after some maneuvering, a car door slammed. Only when the sound of the motor had died away did we dare look at each other and then Hazel, with an air of decision, pulled on a heavy sweater and opened the door.

"Hot coffee and sandwiches for anyone who wants them,"

she called. There were four men, two in the trim uniform of the state police, an older man in plain clothes and a heavy overcoat, and the young bounty-hunter who propped his rifle in a corner and, in response to an inquiry from a policeman, opened his wallet to establish his identity. The policeman scrutinized it carefully, taking his time, and then returned it.

"Not just what you'd expect on a hunting trip," he commented genially. "Lucky for us you were straying on posted land when you found this grave." He was smiling, but he watched the young hunter.

"Actually, it was Miss Barclay who discovered it. She practically fell into it."

"You're not to bother Maggie," Hazel said quickly. "She has had just about all the shock she can take." At her suggestion the men crowded around the dining-room table, on which coffee things had been set out with big plates of sandwiches. They demolished the sandwiches like locusts in a grain field, and drank the hot coffee gratefully.

It was while they were still standing around that Dale's motorcycle roared into sight. Heaven knows he had plenty of warning because of the official cars outside the house. He came in through the kitchen door, his helmet in his hand, looking inquiringly around. For a moment his eyes met those of the young hunter, and then moved on, having asked a question and obtained an answer without a word being spoken.

Recognizing the older man in plain clothes as the leader, Dale asked, "What's going on?"

"Who are you?"

"Dale Curtis. Miss Barclay has kindly let me make use of her garage apartment. Anything wrong?"

"Are you the guy who's been making inquiries around town about a missing caretaker named Prescott?"

"Yes. When Miss Barclay got here several days ago, there

was no trace of him. He seems to have disappeared."

"He's turned up," the younger of the two troopers said laconically. "In a shallow grave in the woods on Miss Barclay's land. Dead a long time, according to the police doctor. Several years probably. That fits, doesn't it?" He looked oddly at Dale.

The latter did not seem to be aware of his open suspicion. "That fits. Was this guy wearing a red flannel shirt and blue jeans?"

"So far as we could tell," the older man cut in.

A bitter flood welled up in my mouth and I ran for the stairs.

When I came back, feeling somewhat limp, the men had gone, after expressing their gratitude to Hazel. Only the young bounty-hunter and Dale remained.

"What about a drink?" Dale suggested.

"That's definitely an idea," the hunter said with alacrity.

Dale turned back from the door and put a heavy package on the table. "I got new locks. I'll put them on before it gets dark."

"Dale, did they say what happened to him?"

"He was shot," the bounty-hunter said, after a glance at Dale. "The bullet fell out when the body decomposed and—"

"Shut up, you fool!" Dale said savagely.

I mixed myself a martini and Hazel forgot her vibrations enough to consent to a small glass of sherry. For a few minutes we sat staring into the blazing fire, sipping our drinks.

"So that," I said at length, "is why someone didn't want me to come back. Because Prescott was buried here."

And at last Hazel reverted to type. "I told you so! I told you it's a house of death."

TEN

"Maggie," Donald said over the telephone, "what is wrong? We've been watching the state police cars and Philippe says something is going on at the house."

"I went out to warn off a man with a rifle who had not noticed the *posted* signs and stumbled into a shallow grave." My voice was shaking, but I could not help it. "The police got the body out and they think, at least it seems to be Prescott, the missing caretaker. He had been shot and he must have been there ever since he disappeared some two years ago."

"My God! What an experience for you."

"It was quite an experience for him too," I said dryly. I looked up as Dale came into the hall.

"Okay if I take the hunter back to the village in the car?"

I nodded and tried to soothe Donald.

"I don't like this at all," he said so solemnly that I found myself laughing.

"That's one way of putting it. But the queer thing is that there seems to be no possible motive for killing the poor fellow. From what we can learn he was a conscientious, honest sort of guy who had no enemies. The people in the

99

village all speak well of him. And it could hardly be the work of thieves. All the valuable paintings were removed and stored at the time my parents died. The silver and crystal and fine china is boxed in the attic."

"I suppose he might have discovered a tramp," Donald suggested.

"Tramps don't usually go around armed. And it's since his death that people in the village have talked about seeing lights, and Dale says someone parked a car in the garage recently. There were fresh oil traces on the floor."

"Dale. That your new tenant?"

"Yes."

"What part did he play in this discovery?"

"He wasn't here. He'd been to the village and didn't get back until after the body had been removed and it was all over."

"What are you going to do now, Maggie? It looks to me as though your house has been used in some rather curious ways."

"I'm staying," I told him, "until I find what this is all about. Prescott was employed by me and he was murdered. And no one has cared enough to find out what happened to him and why."

"Mock-heroics, Maggie?" Donald said gently.

"Maybe. But I'm staying."

Hazel had recuperated from her state of hysteria and she was busy in the kitchen from which the appetizing smell of roasting beef came into the hallway. I drifted back to the living room, looked out at the early darkness, and was relieved when the car lights came in sight. Dale drove the Gremlin into the garage and it was some time before he appeared at the kitchen door.

"I've changed the lock on the garage," he told Hazel. "Mmm. That smells good. I'll do the kitchen door now."

"Would you prefer whipped or baked potatoes?" she asked. "There will be a good rich gravy with the meat."

"Whipped." He worked for a while, said triumphantly, "There you are. I'll leave keys for each of you," and he appeared at the living-room door, where he looked down at me for a moment.

"It all happened a long time ago, Maggie," he said at last, "and it had nothing to do with you."

"Murder concerns everyone, doesn't it?"

"What you need is a martini," he decided. I heard him in the kitchen, joking with Hazel while he mixed martinis, and came back, accompanied by the cheerful sound of ice rattling against the sides of the mixing pitcher. "Well, imagine that," he said in a tone of exaggerated surprise. "I brought two glasses."

However, he filled only one, which he handed me, and then he got to work, putting a new lock on the front door. He squatted down, admiring his work. "That ought to foil the villains," he said in a tone of satisfaction, and then came back to fill the second glass and drop into a chair facing me.

"Well, Maggie, I put in some sound field work today. When Mrs. Williams found your parents, the house was warm. True, there was a gas leak, but the heater was working. Fortunately nothing happened to cause an explosion. Before your couple left for Scotland, a repairman came out to put the heater in the proper condition. It is quite safe now. You understand what that means? The whole story of your father attempting to kill your mother and himself is so much hogwash, to put it bluntly. So why did Hazel tell you such a whopping lie?"

"But she believed it. She said I was the fourth generation. I've thought and thought. But I don't know how to check or where to look. None of my mother's people are alive, and Hazel is the only relation of my father."

101

"Who was your parents' family doctor?"

"I don't know. They were in Washington for two years while my father was in Congress and the only doctor I know of is the heart specialist who was called in when my father had his attack. And the next year I was away at college."

"There have to be records. And if there are records, they can be found. But to repeat: why did Hazel tell you that story about inherited insanity?"

"Because she thought I ought to know."

"Why?"

I shrugged. "Oh, to make me face reality, I guess."

"Anything else?" Dale got up to refill our glasses.

"How tall are you?" I asked irrelevantly.

"Six three. It's a nuisance. No one six foot three can fade into the background."

"Why should you?"

"There are times when it might be convenient. To get back to Hazel—"

He was warning me away from his private affairs though he seemed to have an insatiable curiosity about mine. "Well," I considered, "of course she lost her job a short time ago and she is really up against it. I think she's been hoping that she could have a home with me and maybe she eased her conscience by trying to believe it was I who needed her and not the other way around."

"And where did she get the idea of your heritage in the first place?"

"Gerald. That's why there's got to be some truth in it. Perhaps not about the heater. Thank God you found out about that. But about the heredity."

"Just how much faith do you have in this Gerald?"

"All the faith in the world."

An eyebrow shot up. "When you go out on a limb, you go all the way," Dale said mildly.

"Dale, when you came in this afternoon, when the police were here, you knew that man, didn't you? The fox hunter." When he made no reply, I insisted, "Didn't you?"

"I've come across him now and then in the village."

"But you weren't surprised to find him here."

"Let it go, Maggie. For God sake, let it go."

"I can't let it go. Don't you see that? I've been slow enough. You come to our aid, take care of everything, work your way into this house. We took you on trust."

"If you don't mind my saying so, Maggie, you take too damned many people on trust." Dale looked up as car lights moved across the ceiling, a motor roared and then was shut off. Hazel had come out of the kitchen to join us with her usual cranberry juice when she heard voices and went to switch on the outside lights and open the door on the chain. "Who is it?"

"Terry."

"Oh, no," I groaned under my breath.

Hazel flung open the door and Terry came in, wearing a heavy, almost military-looking brown coat, her hair drawn back severely, wiping snow off her thick glasses and polishing them. She greeted Hazel and walked into the living room, where she took in at a glance the cocktail tray and Dale seated across from me, a glass in his hand. He got up, sustaining her searching look with some amusement. Then she came across the room to me.

"Well, Maggie!"

"How on earth," I exclaimed, more surprised than gracious, "did you get here?"

"Sam drove me up. Mr. Stephens insisted." She was still looking at Dale.

"Terry, this is Dale Curtis. Dale, Miss Tilson of whom you've heard me speak, my trustee's chief assistant."

"We're just about to have dinner," Hazel said. "There's

103

plenty because I have a big roast of beef. I suppose you'd like to have a cocktail while I serve. And I'll prepare the master bedroom for you. It's never been used. As for Sam—"

"I'll fix up the other bed in my quarters for him," Dale offered.

"I'm not spending the night," Terry said. "But it would be nice to have a drink and some dinner. It's been a long cold drive."

Dale took her coat, went out to get another glass, filled it and handed it to her. He glanced at me. "I'll take care of Sam," he said. "Okay?"

"Fine. Thank you."

Terry wore a black dress that was almost like a uniform, with no adornments. She sipped her cocktail for a moment.

"What on earth brought you up here tonight, especially if you don't intend to stay?"

"I can't stay. I have several appointments tomorrow. Mr. Stephens was anxious about you and he was sure you'd soft-pedal anything that was wrong over the telephone, so I thought I'd better see for myself."

"What got Gerald in such a dither?"

"The state police called to check on you, to make sure that you are really Margaret Barclay and that you have been out of the country for the past two years."

"Oh, for heaven's sake!"

"It's not a laughing matter," Terry said. "I understand a dead body was found on your land this afternoon."

I nodded. "We think it was Prescott, and he'd been dead about two years, ever since he disappeared. And he was murdered. Shot. They—found the bullet."

"Prescott! But why on earth—"

"I don't know. But I can't understand why you didn't know he was not receiving his salary."

"I asked my secretary, who said he preferred to be paid by

money order, as he had no bank account." Terry looked at me sharply, almost as though trying to catch me off guard. "I had no idea you had any friends up here."

"You mean Dale Curtis?" Oh, well, it had to be done sooner or later. I told her how he had appeared when we had been in such a state of upheaval, straightened everything up for us, put the house in working order and, because he had no regular job, he had agreed to sleep in the garage apartment so he could be within call and keep an eye on things.

Terry set down her cocktail glass with a click, staring at me through the thick glasses that distorted her eyes. "Really, Maggie! Of all the irresponsible things I ever heard of. You're as mad as the girls who hitchhike, disregarding the horrible risks they run in spite of all the stories about what happens to them. Rape and murder."

I began to laugh.

Terry was not amused. "What do you know about this man? Have you any idea of the chances you are taking, having him around, free to come and go? At least," she added dryly, "so far as I could see when I arrived—very free."

Enough is enough.

"Look here, Terry, let's clear the stage, shall we? You are Gerald's right arm. Fine. But you have never been given the right to interfere in my personal life. You seem to think you have far more authority than you have. But it stops where I am concerned."

She was silent for a moment and my heart thudded. I had never before dreamed of defying her. Then she said, her voice flat, "Of course, it's your life, Maggie. My interest in your welfare is not in the least personal. I don't suppose I've ever liked you any more than you like me. I've watched Mr. Stephens lavish care and devotion on you and you've never made the slightest return. But that's not my business either.

105

I came here because he is extremely worried about you. When he heard that a body had been found on your property, that the police are not satisfied, that they are inquiring about your *bona fides,* he asked me to come up. It's not a trip I'd have chosen on my own. Just one last word. If you needed someone to look out for you, why not call on your tenant, Mr. Gregory? He or his man would willingly look after you, as I gather from what you told me on the telephone."

Hazel appeared in the doorway. "Donald Gregory is a lovely man, but that Philippe is no good. There's an aura—" She saw Terry's expression, sighed, and then said brightly, "Dinner is ready. Just the three of us. Dale took a tray up to his room to share with Sam."

II

After dinner, during which Hazel chattered, stressing how useful she was, cooking, looking after me, seeing that I took care of myself, until anyone would have supposed I was a helpless and hopeless invalid, the subject turned, as it was bound to, to the gruesome discovery of the afternoon.

"How did they ever discover the grave?" Terry asked.

I explained that I had literally fallen into it when I went out to drive a hunter off the posted land.

"What was he doing there?"

"Hunting foxes. There's a bounty on them in Connecticut."

"Of all the freak accidents! And the police have come to no conclusion? They sounded most dissatisfied with the situation when they spoke to Mr. Stephens this afternoon."

"There's no question that it was murder. The puzzle is— why? Everyone had a good word for him. No one would have shot him and buried him just to get his Volkswagen, and there wasn't much else to steal. Things like radios and television sets and typewriters, which dope addicts steal in order to get whatever poison they take, were removed at the time when the house was closed up. But ever since Prescott disappeared there have been rumors, lights seen in an empty house, so that half the village thinks the place is haunted and the other half that it has been an asylum for tramps."

"Of course that's possible," Terry said thoughtfully.

"Except that tramps don't usually come by car, and cars have been in the garage recently, perhaps within a few days. And there were the telephone calls." I told her about the people calling Cincinnati and how Mr. Gregory had settled that by having my number changed.

"Well, there seems to be one level-headed person around here at least. You haven't had strangers coming around, have you?"

"Well, Dale came, but that was to deliver the car, and the hunter who was responsible for our discovering the grave."

Terry on the trail of a fact sounded like a cross-examiner. I told her all I knew about the young hunter except that he and Dale knew each other and Dale had not been surprised to find him there. I didn't know why I held that back. Or perhaps I did.

When she left early, about nine, Hazel and I saw her go without regret. The impeccable Sam, who had not once glanced at me, closed the door of the big Lincoln and it moved off smoothly. I wondered how he felt about my safe arrival in spite of the shortage of gas and the brakes that had been tampered with. I hadn't thought of Sam in some time. Now I wondered what concern it was of his that I should not reach this house? What could he have had to do with Prescott?

Terry had upset me, increasing my own doubts about Dale. Hazel and I washed and put away the dishes almost in silence. Once she said with a sigh, "Terry certainly doesn't make the most of herself, does she? If I had that figure I could look like something." She yawned. "My, this has been an eventful day. I'm going to bed. Of course, I've got my radio, but I do wish I had a nice romance to read, something pleasant where nothing bad ever happens."

"I'm sorry, Hazel. I've been thoughtless. I'll ask Dale to see whether he can pick up a television set. Now that the roads are open, if he can't get anything in Barclaysville, he can go on to Poughkeepsie."

She yawned herself off to bed, carrying her radio, but I was restless and wide awake. The discovery of Prescott's murdered body was bad enough. Terry's unexpected attempt to oust Dale had angered me. More than it should, perhaps. And I was aware that she was justified in pointing out that I had made no return for Gerald's infinite kindness.

That had been a curious interlude when we had spoken to each other, gloves off, and she had been blunt about her dislike of me.

I walked aimlessly around the living room, started upstairs, and heard Hazel splashing in the tub in the bathroom between the two bedrooms. She'd lie there for half an hour, a rubber pillow behind her head, deep in a bubble bath, reading lazily one of the few books she had brought with her, worn copies of love stories of the early days of the century, stories in which nothing unpleasant ever happened or at least in which the reader was comfortably aware that the book would end with a clinch between hero and heroine, who would stroll off into the sunset to live happily ever after.

This reminded me that, tucked away in the attic somewhere, there should be a box of old romances put away years ago because my mother was embarrassed to present the library with anything as undistinguished as *Dorothy Vernon of Haddon Hall* and *The Masquerader*. Hazel would love them.

Grateful to have something to do, I went up to the attic

and browsed around. I found the box of books among a collection of discarded furniture, a box reeking of mothballs containing a valuable tapestry, which my mother had inherited from an ancestor; silver, crystal and china, carefully packed; the original draperies and bedspreads. It was like turning the pages of a memory book.

Up on a rafter and obviously forgotten were my father's binoculars. I took them out of their case, adjusted them and looked out of the window. A square of light came into view. I made another adjustment. A man and woman stood in each other's arms, the woman with dark hair spilling over her naked shoulders, her bare arms linked around the man's neck, her head flung back, his lips on her throat.

When it occurred to me that I was behaving like a peeping Tom, I hastily put away the binoculars, gathered up a few novels for Hazel's delectation, and went to bed. But first I went to check on the new locks on the kitchen and front door. Everything was in shape.

As I got into bed, I found myself thinking of Hazel's distrust of Philippe. I wondered whether Donald was aware of his activities, carried on in his own house; but, perhaps, if he were to keep a virile young man in the country, he had to close his eyes to whatever compensation his servant might require.

I snuggled under the covers, trying to shut out of my mind the memory of that shallow grave, the quick glance exchanged between Dale and the hunter, and Terry's flagrant distrust of Dale.

That night I got colder and colder. Once I even bundled in a dressing gown and went out to the linen closet for more blankets. The hall was like ice, a cold draft swirling around my bare ankles. Perhaps the heater had gone off again. I hesitated at the thought of going down into the basement, but it was more than I could face. I went back, keeping on my warm robe, and piled on blankets. Once I found myself sniffing for gas and scolded myself for a morbid imagination. And then at last I was asleep.

ELEVEN

Next morning I was awakened by the sound of a window being slammed shut. I hurried through the shower and dressed quickly because the room was cold and I thanked heaven that Dale was on hand in case the heater had gone off again.

Hazel was in the kitchen pouring coffee for Dale and asking what he wanted for breakfast. It was obvious that she had been discussing something quite different and had switched the moment she heard me coming. They both turned to look at me.

"This place is freezing," I complained. "Do you think the heater has gone off again?"

"You left the window open in the dining room all night," Hazel said.

"I didn't! How idiotic. I wasn't even in the dining room after we finished the dishes. Whatever gave you such an idea?"

"I heard you prowling all over the house after I went to bed, and the window was wide open when I came downstairs this morning."

"Well, I didn't do it," I told her flatly. "If that window was

111

open, we had a housebreaker last night."

Hazel snorted. "With the snow on the windowsill eight inches deep and untouched? A housebreaker would have had to soar over the windowsill and walk on his hands if he didn't want to leave tracks on the carpet." She gave me a troubled look. "The thing is, Maggie, that you must have done it and just forgotten it."

"Opened a window wide and just forgotten about it with the temperature way below freezing?"

"Terry told me you forgot all about a date with Gerald and went to the Pierre instead of the Plaza. Well, I'll make a nice omelette. I chopped up the leftover ham from the sandwiches. Now don't worry about it, honey. Anyone can do silly things once in a while."

"But I didn't—" I broke off. I might as well have talked to a stone wall. Hazel was sure that I had opened the window, and now I was beginning to wonder. It was true about the mixed-up luncheon appointment. If no one had tried to get in, then why had the window been opened, unless I had done it myself? I pressed my hands to my cheeks, trying to think clearly.

Then Dale spoke for the first time. "What we need here isn't theory, it is nice cold fact, like fingerprints. The trouble is that anyone out of doors last night would have worn gloves."

I looked at him in relief and gratitude. "You think someone else did it?"

"Hold your horses, Maggie. Someone is sawing the lady in half."

"Well, I must say," Hazel sputtered, "if you think I had anything to do with this—"

"I don't," Dale assured her. "I'd just put you down as a case of brainwashing."

Which meant, didn't it, that he believed Gerald had convinced Hazel, for reasons I could not conceive, that I had a streak of insanity in my makeup? And I refused to believe it.

"Well, I must say—"

"Aw, Hazel, don't be like that," Dale said cajolingly. "What about that omelette? I'm famishing."

She beat the egg whites until they were stiff, folded in the yolks and the ham, and poured the mixture into a buttered pan, tilting it slightly from side to side while it browned. Dale busied himself making toast, pouring juice, and refilling the coffee cups.

"How did you make out with the impenetrable Sam?" I asked him.

Dale chuckled. "That really had its comic aspect. We were scrupulously polite, but he was trying to pump me and I was trying to pump him."

"Did you say anything in regard to the car he had bought for me and was supposed to have gone over inch by inch?"

"I did indeed. That got really under his skin. He swore that there was nothing wrong at the time when he examined it and he had put it in the garage where Mr. Stephens kept his Lincoln, a couple of blocks away. He intends to find out who was on duty that night and who could have tampered with the car. He was all worked up about it."

"Did you believe him?"

Dale hesitated and I felt that he was making up his mind what to say. "He gave me the impression that he was completely loyal to Mr. Stephens, who had given him a chance to rebuild his life and had treated him with complete confidence."

"Oh?"

"Well, there's no evidence either way. For what it's worth, he came near convincing me. We had a long talk about it,

113

chewing the whole thing over, considering possibilities."

"But if it wasn't Sam who tampered with the brakes and who attacked me—"

"That poses a problem, doesn't it? I'd made it clear that you had been mugged right outside the house and that you were damned near throttled. I made no accusations, but he was on it like a flash. He said he'd spent the evening playing poker with some cronies of his. Four to seven guys who meet when they can in a crummy little room over a delicatessen. The guy who owns the place provides free beer and pretzels. He and Sam seem to be the only two with a local habitation and a name. The rest are a fluctuating crowd whom it would be hard to pin down, and unreliable as witnesses for an alibi."

Hazel had divided the fluffy omelette with forks, slid it on our plates. Then Dale raised his hands above his head and shook hands with himself, beaming at Hazel, who beamed back.

"What did Sam want to know about you?" I asked.

"He wasn't as direct as that. Neither of us was. We played a much more delicate game, Miss Barclay," Dale assured me with dignity. "Finesse. Rapiers, not bludgeons. He wanted to know how I'd become a member of the household, in a manner of speaking. I explained," he smiled in a kindly way, "that I had agreed to stay on here only because it was obvious to the meanest intelligence that two helpless women needed a competent male to look after them."

"I could hit you, Dale!"

"But," and he was serious now, "I gave him a fairly complete picture of the situation you found here, including the dead rat. Even to Sam it added up to a deliberate attempt to drive you away. And the discovery that Prescott had been murdered and buried on the premises two years ago was the clincher. Whatever this house has been used for, it is serious

114

enough to be worth risking murder. There's no statute of limitations on murder."

"What did Sam say about that?"

"He said several things: one was that his boss would probably either have a fit or come up himself or send Sam to keep an eye on you because you were of considerable importance to him. Another was that he disliked intensely his boss's trusted assistant, Theresa Tilson. He practically froths at the mouth when he mentions her."

"That's mutual," I said. "Terry thinks Gerald made a terrible mistake and took a risk in hiring an ex-convict."

Dale stretched out long fingers for another piece of toast. "And what else did Sam have to say?"

"Well, this and that. Sam is no fool, you know, except where women are concerned, and he seems to have learned his lesson there. We talked over ways and means."

So he wasn't going to talk. To me, at least. I knew when I was beaten. After breakfast he stood looking at the window that had been opened the night before. As Hazel had pointed out, there were no marks on the sill where the snow was untouched, no indications that anyone could have climbed in. But someone could have stood on a box and raised the window, which was unlocked.

"It seems so pointless," I said.

"Unless someone wants to convince you that you do irrational things," Dale said soberly. "Make you so uncertain of yourself that you'll flee to the security of Gerald Stephens."

"Which means Hazel. There's no one else here to do such a thing."

"I won't buy Hazel. There has to be someone else. If you don't need anything, I'll run into the village. I'm out of cigarettes."

"You might look around and see whether there's any-

115

where to rent a television set for Hazel."

"Okay."

I went upstairs to do what I should have done in the beginning—move into the master bedroom. I stripped my bed and made up one in the bigger room, wondering why I had shied away from it, a square gracious room with a soft gold carpet. Somewhere in the attic were gold satin quilted covers for the twin beds. When I had made them both up, the room should look very nice. I recalled that my mother had usually kept a vase of flowers on the table beside the chaise longue, from which I stripped the dust cover, and that she kept a hanging plant at the window. I went to check whether the heavy chain was still there.

Walking past the house was a young man in a ski outfit, skis strapped on his back, poles in his hands, plodding toward the top of the slope behind the house. I remembered how as a twelve-year-old I had gone down that slope with other youngsters of my own age, from one of whom I had borrowed skis. Mother had put a stop to it, saying that if I wanted to ski, she would take me to Vermont or New Hampshire during winter weekends, where I could learn from a proper instructor. And, she implied, in the proper company. But we never went. I still remembered the exhilaration of skimming down the slope. Like flying.

As I watched the solitary skier, Dale came out, wheeling his motorcycle, helmet in hand. For a moment the two men chatted, Dale looming over the other man, and then, after a quick glance at the house that sent me instinctively ducking behind the heavy dark draperies, he handed him a box of cigarettes, got on his bike and was off with a roar.

After a few minutes the young man came down on his skis, over which he had no control whatsoever. He hooked one behind the other, went head over heels in the snow, skis flying in air. He sat up, looking disgusted, and trudged on down the slope on foot. He did not return for another try. I stood there for a long time. One thing was clear. I'd have to ask Dale to go. He had lied about the cigarettes. Lied pointlessly. There was no reason why he had to explain his actions to me. So why?

By the time I had moved my clothes and my cosmetics, put things away in drawers or hung them in Mother's closet, lined with some quilted yellow material, I got out matching yellow towels for the yellow bathroom and rummaged for scented soap. In the attic I unearthed the satin covers for the twin beds and when everything was in shape, I looked around with pleasure and with no sense of uneasiness about sleeping in this room. It had the kind of handsome opulence that had been so much a part of Mother's personality, but it no longer overwhelmed me.

A cough made me turn to the door where Hazel was watching me arrange pillows on the chaise longue.

"I thought we'd be more comfortable if we each had our own bath," I explained.

"I wondered why you hadn't done that before unless you were afraid of the room and its associations." Hazel looked around. "It's beautiful, isn't it? At least when you can forget what happened here."

I refused to recognize the gambit. "It will be beautiful when we get rid of those heavy draperies. You know, Hazel, I've been thinking about them. We never had anything like that. It's as though someone had wanted to conceal any lights, though the house was supposed to be unoccupied. Let's get Dale to take them down for us. The original drapes are packed in the attic. When we put them up, the whole house will be lighter and more pleasant."

"What made you go prowling around last night?" Hazel asked.

"I remembered that a lot of romantic novels had been

117

packed away up there," I improvised, "and I thought you might enjoy them. I brought them down for you but left them in the other bedroom. If you like them, there's a whole box full, probably thirty or forty novels."

"Oh, goody!" Hazel exclaimed, with one of her unfortunate lapses into girlishness. She went into the room I had left to get the books, greeting them with little squeals of delight.

Dale did not come back for lunch, but the state police called to ask for the address of the Browns who had lived so long in the twin house. I told them I had no idea. My trustee —that was Mr. Gerald Stephens of the Stephens Importing firm?—yes—had said they had gone out to California to live with one of their children, but I had no idea where. Why did they want the Browns?

"Living that close to your house, Miss Barclay, they may have been aware of any unusual activities there. After all, the road leads only to the two houses. We get a lot of talk in the village and, though you can usually disregard rumors, most of it seems to be fairly consistent, especially the business of the lights. The house is on the highest point, you know. Also it is conceivable the Browns can pinpoint more accurately the time of the disappearance of your caretaker, Prescott."

"I'm sure you are wrong about that," I told the trooper. "As I remember them the Browns are simply monuments of integrity. If they had the faintest suspicion that anything was wrong, they would never in the world have kept it to themselves for fear of involvement. They are terribly responsible people."

"Well, that's helpful. But you have no idea where to reach them?"

"Probably Terry—Miss Tilson, my guardian's assistant— would know. She handled the renting of the twin house."

"Everything all right there now?" the trooper asked casually.

"Fine, thank you." Belatedly, I exclaimed, "Good heavens, you don't expect to find any more bodies, do you?"

He laughed at that. "I hope not. You can always reach me if you need me."

"Thank you, but I hope the necessity won't arise."

The next call was from Gerald. "What in God's name is this that Terry has been telling me?"

"About Prescott, you mean?"

"No, I got all that from the state police. I mean this fellow you've picked up out of nowhere and taken in. Have you gone out of your mind, Maggie?"

"Is that what you think, Gerald?" I asked as quietly as I could.

"What's that? Oh, don't be absurd. It's not like you to be so literal. But Terry tells me the fellow is quite at home there, having cocktails with you, calling you Maggie."

"Terry takes quite an interest in my affairs."

"I think," Gerald said after a pause, "perhaps she is taking an interest in my affairs." I could hear the hurt in his voice.

"Please don't worry, Gerald. Please. Remember that Hazel is here and no one ever had a more determined chaperon."

"Sorry. I didn't mean to harass you, my dear. Or pry. Would you think I am encroaching too much on your private life," and there was unexpected humility in his voice, "if I suggest that Sam go up there for a week or so, or as long as you need him?"

"No," I said sharply, "I won't have that man around. I've never trusted him, Gerald. You know that."

"So I gathered from Terry. She seems to think you believe he was responsible for the attack on you the night before you left here. Why in God's name didn't you tell me yourself, Maggie? Have you lost all confidence in me since that illtimed proposal?"

119

"No, Gerald, of course not. There's no one in the world whom I trust so completely or of whom I'm so fond."

"Then that should satisfy me, shouldn't it? Who could be unreasonable enough to ask for more? Good-bye, my dear."

Hazel, who disliked being left out of things, was hovering in the doorway while I talked to Gerald. "Well, what was that all about?" Then, fortunately, her attention was distracted. "Goodness, who do you know who drives a Bentley? I wish you'd look, Maggie. Cream-colored, simply gorgeous, and about the size of a freight car."

The car slid noiselessly to a stop and Philippe went to open the door and assist Donald Gregory, handing him his crutch and guiding him safely over the walk Dale had cleared earlier.

"Heavens, I didn't even put on any lipstick!" Hazel exclaimed as she ran for the stairs.

I opened the door. "Donald! Should you be out on a day like this?"

"Of course. I just have to watch my step." He came in and nodded to Philippe. "Come back for me—" He looked at me questioningly. "May I stay for a while?"

"As long as you like. We'll be delighted."

"Shall we say an hour then?" As he seated himself in a deep chair, his leg stretched out before him, his crutch within reach, his hands in their rubber gloves resting lightly on one knee, he looked around. "How charming this is!" Today the scars on his face were less obvious. "Well, you've had more than you asked for, haven't you? What a horrible discovery! What do the police make of it?"

"So far I don't think they have any particular theory. At least they aren't confiding in me and I know they checked with my trustee to find out for sure that I'd been out of the country for the past two years. But from what I gathered when they called me today, they seem to believe this house

120

was used for some sort of illegal enterprise, and they are trying to get in touch with the Browns, who rented your house until you moved in, thinking they may have noticed something, at least narrow down the time when Prescott disappeared. That's about all. It's a shame, when you came here to recuperate, that you should find yourself in the midst of all this melodrama."

"Just on the periphery," he said. "They came to talk to me this morning but, of course, we'd arrived long after the fact, so we were of no use to them."

He struggled to his feet as Hazel came in. She had changed to a red dress that added pounds to her weight and she was freshly made-up. Again she had applied a lavish amount of my perfume.

"Oh, don't get up," she exclaimed. "You mustn't put too much weight on that poor leg of yours. Is there any permanent bone damage?"

There was no stopping Hazel when her curiosity was aroused. Donald gave her his charming smile. "Doctors are rarely specific about what is permanent. Haven't you noticed?"

"I don't believe in doctors myself," Hazel said. "But if you have any pain, I know a marvelous man who performs acupuncture."

Donald's lips twitched. "How kind you are, but for the time being I don't need such extreme measures." He turned to me. "I hope you haven't been troubled by any more nuisance calls."

"Thanks to you, they stopped as soon as the number was changed. But it was a queer business, the word Cincinnati being used as a sort of code."

"Code?" Hazel pounced. "You do get the craziest ideas."

Donald smiled. "But they make life more interesting, don't they?"

121

Hazel had no patience with this sort of talk. "Would you like some coffee?"

"No, thank you."

"There's some sherry," she persisted. "Some sherry and perhaps some crackers and cheese. Something to nourish you. I think when people are recuperating they need a lot of little snacks, don't you?"

Bowing to the inevitable, Donald agreed to sherry and Hazel bustled out happily. Donald's lips twitched as he looked at me. "Your cousin takes as much care of me as Philippe does. He's the original faithful watchdog."

"Well, not all the time," I said, and laughed.

He was surprised. "What do you mean?"

I described finding my father's binoculars the night before, trying them out, and seeing Philippe holding a woman in a passionate embrace.

Donald looked startled. "Philippe! You're sure?"

"Oh, perfectly sure. Of course, when it dawned on me that I was behaving like a peeping Tom, I put away the glasses."

"I suppose it's possible. As a rule I go to bed early. And I know he has a fiancée who works somewhere in the vicinity. I imagine that was his chief inducement to take the job."

"Judging by what I saw, I'll bet she works as a topless waitress."

Donald laughed at that. "Well, if she is Philippe's escape from reality, more power to him. I wonder how he managed to smuggle her in so quietly?" He laughed again and shook his head. Then he looked down at the stiff leg. "It's possible I've overlooked the fact that Philippe is a normal man." There was bitterness in his tone.

And then Hazel came in with the sherry decanter, glasses, a plate of crackers, three kinds of cheese, and some biscuits covered with an evil-smelling purple dip of her own manufacture. Donald gamely sampled some of everything and steered the conversation onto my foreign travels, giving her no further opportunity to pursue her personal observations.

As Philippe appeared with the Bentley promptly at the end of the hour, Donald asked, "Is everything working all right now? The electricity? The heater?"

"Oh, the heater's all right," Hazel said, "but last night Maggie left a window wide open in the dining room and we nearly froze. At least I didn't, because I always have my electric blanket with me, but the house was like ice this morning."

"I keep telling you I did nothing of the kind," I said wearily, and went to open the door for Philippe.

Expressionless, except for the slightly sullen droop of his lips, there was nothing to suggest the impassioned lover of the night before. As he helped Donald into his overcoat and gave him his crutch, the latter said, "Thank you for letting me come. It is a pleasant break after that empty house."

"Come whenever you like," Hazel said. "Except for Terry we haven't seen a soul and it gets lonely. I hope we're not settled here for the rest of the winter, Maggie. I miss my bridge nights and my television programs, especially now that I'm not working and there are such lovely daytime shows."

"I asked Dale to look around and see if he can find a set," I told her.

"Who did open that window?" Donald asked me in a low voice.

"I wish to God I knew!"

"Don't let it worry you."

"I won't," I assured him as he began his cautious walk to the car.

TWELVE

Dale did not come back for dinner; it must have been about ten when the motorcycle roared up and I heard the garage door close. I stole into the empty bedroom and looked out to see light flash on in the living room of the garage apartment.

It must have been about one o'clock when I became aware that I was chilled, the sheets felt icy, and my nose and ears were cold. If someone was playing games, sawing the lady in half, I was going to find out about it. Without giving myself time to panic, I ran down the stairs, guiding myself with my hand on the railing.

As soon as I reached the bottom, I felt the icy draft on my bare ankles. The dining-room window was open again. Noiselessly I went into the dark room and for a moment I stood very still, so still that near me I could hear the faint sound of cloth brushing against cloth as someone moved. Whatever threatened me was not coming from outside but from within the house. And then someone knocked against me, hurling me off my feet, and I fell over a dining-room chair and brought up against the corner cupboard, striking my head against it with the full force of my fall.

Someone was moving fast now, making no attempt to be quiet; there was the sound of grunts, of trampling feet. On hands and knees I crawled toward the door, straightened up, and found the light switch. For a moment I stood leaning against the wall, dizzy from the blow I had got on my head, half blinded by the sudden light. The window, as I had supposed, was wide open and beside it, leaning out, was Dale, fully dressed except for soft slippers, a revolver in his hand.

"You?" I said numbly at last.

"He got away," Dale said quickly.

"And you just happened to be here, in the house, and armed?"

"No, I was waiting. I thought something like this might happen. Not the gun, of course, but another attempt to undermine your faith in your own sanity."

"That's not your gun?"

"Good God! I took it away when I grappled with the fellow. It was like trying to hold an eel. He didn't want to fight, just to get away."

"So there really was an intruder?"

Dale came to put a hand on my shoulder and it tightened when I tried to move away. "There really was an intruder. Don't you believe me?"

I looked toward the window with the snow blowing in. "How can I tell?" I said dully. "By daylight, after a storm like this, there will be no trace of a housebreaker."

"And you can't take me on trust?" Dale's lips twisted in mute disappointment, and then he stood turning the revolver over and over in his hand.

"Give it to me," I said. "I'm going to turn it over to the police in the morning."

He held it out, saying only, "Careful! It's loaded."

"How do you know?"

"Because I think tonight you were going to go berserk and

kill yourself. Part of the old family curse. Here's Hazel all primed to explain to the police about your heredity. It's a natural setup. For God's sake, go back to New York tomorrow." He added, his manner remote, "After, of course, you've talked to the police and turned over the evidence. Now you'd better go back to bed. I'll be here all night, though I don't think he'll come back, knowing I am on the spot."

"And having you in the house should reassure me?"

"What is this, Maggie? What's got into you?"

"Did you remember to buy some cigarettes in the village, Dale?"

"Oh!" He caught his breath. Then he grinned. "So that's it. You saw me pass a furtive message to a mysterious stranger."

"Don't talk like that. You make it sound so silly."

"Actually that is just about what happened. Sorry I was so obvious about it and worried you."

"Worried me! Dale, I want you to give me your keys and tomorrow I want you to go."

He came very close to me and I felt a moment of panic when he loomed over me. And then he said abruptly, "I can take just so much," and I was crushed in his arms, while he kissed me. Only then did I recall that I was wearing nothing but a practically transparent nightgown.

With the same abruptness he released me. "Forgive me if you can, though I can't say I am sorry." He fumbled in his pocket and pulled out the keys to the house and the garage, put them on the table beside the revolver. Then he went over to close the window and fumble uselessly with the broken lock.

"Dale, did you search the apartment of the twin house while Hazel and I were having dinner there?"

"Yeah." No explanation, just the word as though it should be enough to satisfy me.

"Breaking and entering. That's a felony, isn't it? Not just a misdemeanor. If you were charged with that, you'd have to face trial. Why are you doing things like that?"

"Look, my darling, if you stay around here any longer looking like that, I won't be answerable for the consequences. Anyhow, it's late for a heart-to-heart. Let it go until tomorrow."

"Can't you explain anything?" It was almost a wail of frustration.

"All I can tell you right now is that you just happened to step into something and got in the way. You remember I told you in the beginning that my coming here was part of the job. That's all I can say at the moment. I hoped—there was something building between us, Maggie, something real. I could feel it and I'm sure you could too. There's no mistaking the real thing. I hoped you'd trust me."

"But, Dale, just blind trust, blind faith; that's a lot to ask, isn't it?"

"If it is, then I've made a big mistake," he said soberly. He covered my hand with his. "Maggie," he began urgently, and then he released me, snatched up the revolver and keys, dropped them in his pocket and was three feet away from me when Hazel's mules came clattering down the stairs.

She wore a cap tied under her chin to hold her wave in place and her face was thick with some heavy cream. In one hand she held a slipper with a high heel, apparently to be used as a weapon. She stared at us for a moment.

"Well!" she said. "I'm sure I'm sorry to disturb you."

I could hardly blame her.

"Hazel, someone opened the window again and Dale was

watching to see who was playing tricks and nearly caught him, but the man got away."

"It's all right now," Dale said quickly, picking up his cue. "I'll be on duty the rest of the night."

"You mean Maggie didn't really open it? Dressed like that, she just wandered downstairs for nothing?"

"She really didn't," Dale assured her. "The intruder had opened the window before she came down to investigate."

"Well, I'm relieved to know that. And it's mighty nice of you to sit up. You'd better go to bed, Maggie. Really! Not even a dressing gown." To Dale she offered her usual panacea for all ills. "Would you like some coffee?"

"Nothing, thank you, unless you have something to read."

"With the exception of some old-fashioned novels, all the books were left to the local library after my parents died," I said.

Hazel sniffed. "I'll bring you something. As for being old-fashioned—just because there's nothing—well, unpleasant, if you know what I mean." She went upstairs.

"That's my girl," Dale said softly.

"I'm not—"

"Oh, yes, you are." He broke off as Hazel came clattering down. She held out a book. As she and I went back to bed, Dale settled down at the dining-room table with a copy of *Lavender and Old Lace.*

II

When I came down to breakfast the next morning, I found Dale sprawled out in the dining room, his arms on the table and his head on his arms, a tuft of hair standing up on the crown of his head. In sleep his face had an oddly defenseless look, the mouth more vulnerable. I found myself staring down at him for a long time. At length I suppose that unswerving gaze aroused him and he opened his eyes. For a

128

moment he blinked sleepily and then he stretched out one hand toward me. I wanted to put mine in it; instead, I said austerely, because events were moving too fast for me, "You'd better go over to your own apartment and get some proper sleep."

"I've had all the sleep I need. But I'd better shower and shave before I face Hazel for breakfast."

Neither of us referred to my demand the night before that he go away. Anyhow the snow had left us completely sealed in for the day.

As we heard Hazel's door open, Dale said quickly, "I've got to talk to you, Maggie."

"After breakfast you can get a ladder from the basement and take down all those heavy draperies and help me hang the ones that are up in the attic."

"Right. Back in fifteen minutes."

Hazel came in as the door closed behind Dale. She looked disappointed. "I thought I heard voices."

"Poor Dale! He sat up all night. I just found him asleep and sent him off to shave before breakfast."

"I'm going to make waffles and I got some of those little sausages. It will take twenty minutes for breakfast. But we're going to need more supplies. When we shopped, I wasn't figuring on having a man to feed. Though I must say it makes cooking more rewarding, doesn't it?"

Absently I picked up the copy of *Lavender and Old Lace*. Hardly Dale's kind of reading material. The book fell open at the beginning of Chapter Two, where the place had been marked by an envelope thrust carelessly into the book. It was addressed to Mr. Dale Curtis at the Hotel Carlyle in New York and written in green ink in a flowing hand, a feminine hand. I was about to toss it into the wastebasket when I felt an enclosure inside. I would not, of course, have taken the letter out of the envelope, but what I did was just as inexcus-

129

able. I held it up to the light and read easily the words on the single sheet:

Dale, darling, I can't endure this any longer. I do need you so terribly. I've changed my mind. I'll do anything you say. Anything. My love to you. Isabelle.

I looked at the envelope again and tried to make out the date, but it was smudged.

It wasn't necessary to say anything when Dale came in to breakfast, because Hazel was voluble enough for both of us. She demanded to know just what had happened, what kind of fight Dale had had with the intruder, and how he had got away and where he could conceivably have gone in a storm like that. No one could live long out in the night and the snow and the freezing cold. And she hadn't heard a car. Anyhow she was glad it was someone else, even if it was a tramp or a burglar. Anything was better than Maggie—you know—getting fancies or anything.

After breakfast Dale began taking down the heavy draperies and Hazel decided that she might as well do up the window curtains at the same time. But Dale didn't need a ladder. He was tall enough to reach the heavy draperies easily.

"These have been up some time," he said. "The linings are stained from rain." As he dropped the first one on the floor, a little cloud of dust went up, making us sneeze. When Hazel had gathered up the curtains and gone down to put them through the washing machine, Dale said, "Someone sure wanted to have a blackout here. With the house standing above the village as it does, lights would be a dead giveaway. No wonder they weren't always successful. On a dark night

130

people inside might not notice they hadn't been closed tight."

"But what were they up to? You know, don't you?"

"I'm virtually positive. The only thing is that I haven't a scrap of tangible proof."

"Except for Prescott being shot and buried in the woods," I pointed out. "Did he—have anything to do with whatever it was?"

Dale faced me then, holding heavy drapes in his arms. "No, I think he just happened to get in the way. Like you." He dropped the drapes on top of the others and we both sneezed.

"I guess that's the lot," he said. "Do you want them stored in the attic?"

"No, I don't want them. Better have them cleaned and put them in a Good Will box. Someone can use them."

He nodded. "I'll take them to the village cleaner as soon as we can get out," and he nodded toward the window. It was one of those days in early February when country people in Connecticut stay home because they can't get out.

"Snowbound," he said thoughtfully. "In certain circumstances that's a wonderful idea. But," as the electric washer began to churn, "there are drawbacks."

I was wise enough to ignore any suggestion that he and I would find elysium in being snowbound.

As he followed me up to the attic to get the original drapes for the windows, I said as casually as I could, "Oh, this must belong to you. You used it as a bookmark in Hazel's novel."

"Wonderfully soporific," he said, glanced at the envelope, and slipped it into the pocket of the flannel shirt he was wearing, a dark blue flannel, beautifully cut and fitting his broad shoulders as though it had been tailored for him, as it probably was.

131

"What are you up to, Dale?" I asked when the attic door had closed behind us.

"Right now I'm at a standstill. You could help me, if you would."

"Why should I?" This was foolish and he did not attempt to answer it. He looked at me, his eyes smiling. Then I remembered the letter. *I'll do anything you say.* Well, that might be his loving Isabelle's decision. It wasn't mine.

I opened the big box and began to remove the draperies. When the silence had been prolonged uncomfortably, Dale said, "I need your help, Maggie. I want to know about the setup in the twin house. I've checked in the village. According to everyone I've talked to, this chap Gregory moved in shortly after the Browns left, only a few days before you did. He's just out of a hospital and new around here. But that man of his, Philippe Thibault, has been around for some time. He never seems to hold a job, at least in the vicinity, but he appears to have plenty of money to spend. I'm as interested as hell in friend Philippe."

"Why?"

Dale nodded out of the attic window. "Hazel made sense for once in her life when she said a man couldn't live long in last night's storm. And where else could he go without a car?"

"You think Philippe is the one who has been making this house his headquarters? Do you think Philippe killed Prescott?"

"If you can think of anyone else who could have pulled that trick about the open window, you're way ahead of me."

"Hazel has said from the beginning that she does not trust him, that there was something familiar about him." I laughed. "The only thing I know—" and I told Dale about finding my father's binoculars, turning them on the lighted window in the twin house, and seeing a half-naked woman

132

in Philippe's passionate embrace. Donald had seemed to be amused when I told him about it, and said he understood Philippe had a fiancée who worked in the neighborhood, which was probably why he had taken the job.

"You think he was smuggling in this female without Gregory knowing about it?"

I nodded. "I imagine Donald was more envious than shocked. He looks as though he has been through a lot. He was in some explosion, and he's lame and has to use a crutch and I imagine he was quite horribly burned. You can see the scars on his head and he wears gloves to hide some deformity, about which Hazel insists on talking. She even wanted to read his palm. Honestly, Dale, there are times—"

He nodded. "Poor devil, that must be rough. Well, it's a cinch he wasn't our housebreaker last night."

"Good heavens, what an idea! He's one of the most delightful men I've ever met. Hazel has capitulated completely to his charms."

"You too?"

I'll do anything you say. I remembered that curious meeting with the non-skier and Dale handing over a box of cigarettes which might or might not conceal a message. I remembered the tacit recognition between Dale and the man who had been responsible for the discovery of Prescott's grave. I remembered the brakes that had failed and the thumbs that had pressed cruelly into my throat. But they had nothing to do with each other. They couldn't have. Could they? I didn't want it to be Dale who was behind all that horror.

At last I said tentatively, "Dale, could there possibly be an association between Sam and Philippe?"

"Sam? Oh, your trustee's chauffeur. Well, now, that's a combination I hadn't thought of. It could account for a lot of things. And yet I'll swear the guy struck me as completely trustworthy and truthful when he expressed his gratitude to

Stephens. He was ready to do anything for him."

"That's the effect Gerald has on people. He's completely splendid, Dale. The finest human being I've ever known."

"Them is big words, lady."

"I mean them."

"I know you do." Dale picked up the drapes, managing the whole lot without difficulty. "Shall we get these hung?" As I started down the attic stairs, he said, "I'm going to New York tomorrow. I may be gone a couple of days. Will you be all right? I'll leave the revolver with you and fix the windows so no one can get in without breaking the glass, which is not what is wanted. You'll be all right."

"Of course we'll be all right," I said, trying to sound as though I meant it.

"Maggie," he said as I started to open the attic door, "can I come back?"

I showed him in which rooms the drapes were to go and watched him hang them. As he finished the last ones in the living room and stood back to admire his handiwork, I said, as though there had been no long interval, "Yes, you can come back."

As Hazel came in to exclaim at the difference and praise Dale for his work, I went up to my room. I might not be insane, I told myself grimly, but I was a damned fool.

THIRTEEN

That afternoon the sun came out, the temperature rose from twenty to forty-five, and there was a feeling of spring in the air, a typical early February thaw.

I began the tedious business of putting in a call to the MacTavishes somewhere in Scotland and the Browns somewhere in California. This involved calling Terry to get their addresses, and I dreaded her insistent questions about my reason for calling them. To my relief I got her secretary, who said Miss Tilson was out of the office on business and could not be reached. When I explained what I wanted, she found, without difficulty, the address of the MacTavishes in Edinburgh. There was a considerable delay in finding the address of the Browns. Finally the secretary said, "May I call you back, Miss Barclay? I seem to have misfiled the address of the Browns."

There was an unaccustomed rumble and I looked out of the window. Any activity on a country road during a big storm is bound to attract attention. The snowplow was going past, followed by the sander. When the two cumbersome vehicles had maneuvered around the narrow turn at the top

135

and returned, Dale came in wearing his heavy jacket and gloves, helmet in his hand.

"Now the road is clear, I am going to New York. I'll make it back as quickly as I can, but it may be a couple of days. If you should need anything and want to reach me, call 212-CI 7-4346. Ask for Mrs. William Fillmore. Got that?"

Like a fool I said, "Or shall I ask for Isabelle?"

He stopped short and his face hardened. At length he said, "If you like." He went out and in a few minutes I saw the motorcycle headed down the hill toward the village and New York and Isabelle. He did not turn to wave.

Sometime later Terry's secretary called to give me the address of the Browns in Santa Barbara. "Of all things," she said apologetically, "I must have put it in Miss Tilson's private file. And I've never touched it before!"

Night had fallen in Scotland when I reached the Mac-Tavishes. It was, I suppose, the first call they had ever received from overseas, and they were so surprised and delighted that it took time to get to my question.

I went through all the usual platitudinous routine of "How nice it is to hear your voice." At length I broke in to tell them bluntly the rumor I had heard about the heater and my father's suspected action and the reason for it.

Mr. MacTavish stuttered in sheer rage and finally said, "Here, Mother, you take this." And I heard him give her a hasty summary of the situation.

"Miss Maggie," she exclaimed, "it's a wicked lie. Never believe a word of it. I don't know what mischief-maker dreamed up a story like that. The heater was a bit unreliable but it worked. It was repaired a few times but now and then there was trouble with escaping gas. It was the gas that caused the trouble, of course, but the heater was working. The house was warm. I'd swear to it. We were surprised when they were late coming down to breakfast, but we never suspected it was the gas. We'd noticed it downstairs, of course, and opened windows to clear it out. But then it was too late, even if we'd gone up then.

"Your father was the nicest gentleman who ever lived and that gentle! And Mrs. Barclay—well, a very firm sort of lady in her way and knew what she wanted. But she was no more insane than I am. And when it comes to any insanity in the family—well, there! I remember when you were a little lassie away at that school of yours, I went with your mother because your grannie had caught an infection. It was an epidemic of some sort and no nurses to be had. Your grannie was in Reno at the time, getting her second divorce. A very frivolous woman for her age, very social, just back from Cannes where she had been gambling. Middle fifties and sane as sane. If you need anyone to testify, I'll come and on my own money, too, considering the way the Master provided for us.

"And as for your great-grannie, they spoke of her at the time. More like your mother she'd have been and she disapproved of her frivolous daughter. Something of a tartar she sounded like, if you'll forgive my saying so. Just remember, Miss Maggie, what you've been told is a wicked lie."

I answered her anxious questions about my health and welfare and assured her everything was just fine.

"I don't like to think of you being alone up there," said the kindly troubled voice with its pronounced Scotch accent, which had intensified now she was back in her native environment. "Of course you've got the Browns to call on, and nicer people you'll never find."

I didn't think it wise to tell her the Browns had gone away, but I said my cousin Hazel was with me.

Mrs. MacTavish sniffed at this. "And there she'll stay as

137

long as you let her. Your mother would invite her now and then, but she'd always make clear what the day to depart was and abide by it."

I laughed at that and assured her that I was in control of the situation and I hope I never again tell as big a lie.

The next call was to the Browns in California. They were just finishing lunch and Mrs. Brown told me, in the gloating tone of people who bask in sunshine while the Northeast freezes, that they had had their lunch out of doors after a refreshing dip in the pool.

"You'll wonder why I am disturbing you," I said, "but something rather upsetting has come up. Do you remember Prescott, our caretaker?"

"Of course. He seemed so reliable. I wondered at the time he left why you had not replaced him."

"Do you remember exactly when he went away? This is important, Mrs. Brown."

"Well, I—" There was a pause. "It must have been about two years ago. I know it was in winter."

"You couldn't pinpoint it?"

"I don't see how. Oh, wait! My husband had to have some dental work done and we expected to spend a week in Boston and we went to ask Prescott if he'd watch our house, but apparently he had just packed up and left. His clothes were gone and there was no sign of him in the apartment. Just a minute— Horace, when did you have that upper plate remade in Boston? . . . Oh, that's right, it was Valentine's Day, because he looked so ridiculous coming into the hotel bringing me a great bunch of red tulips and no upper teeth."

"That's a big help," I said.

"You know we wondered afterwards because there were goings on we didn't like."

"What things?"

"Well, lights in the house where no one was supposed to

138

be. Just cracks of light as though the drapes had been drawn. Horace always walks morning and night and he frequently passed your house and even in the mornings those dark drapes were closed and in the evenings he could see slits of light. You know how light shows up on a dark country night? And now and then he'd see a car in the garage and often he'd hear the phone ring while he was walking past, and it never rang more than a couple of times, so someone must have answered it."

"Did you report any of this to the police?"

"Horace said it would make us look like busybodies and maybe Mr. Stephens wouldn't like it if we interfered, but we did report it to him, of course. We said we felt the house was being used for some illicit purpose and that Prescott was not there any more."

"You told Mr. Stephens that?"

Mrs. Brown sounded surprised at the shock in my voice. "Why, yes, of course. Well, actually, we talked to Miss Tilson, but she said she'd relay our message to Mr. Stephens and there was nothing to worry about. Prescott had gone on to a job that offered better pay and better opportunities for advancement."

"Prescott," I said, when I could command my voice, "was shot to death at the time he disappeared. Day before yesterday his body was discovered in a shallow grave in the woods behind my house."

"Oh, how awful!"

"There's another thing, Mrs. Brown. You knew my parents for a long time." I told her the whole thing, the version of their death I had been told and the story of my heritage of insanity.

"That, my dear, is vicious nonsense," she said emphatically. "I won't pretend that your mother was not a dominating woman, but in her own way she did a lot of good. And

139

my husband and I met her mother in Monaco. She looked a lot like you with your charm and your gaiety, when you let yourself go. She was married to her third husband then. And she told me some hilarious stories about *her* mother, your great-grandmother, who lived to be ninety and was a holy terror, and fired any servant who took a drink or failed to go to church on Sunday. She was in full control of herself up to the day she died, when she made the only jest of her life. She said she wanted on her tombstone: 'She thought she knew best.' You can't help admiring a woman like that. If anyone tells you any more outrageous lies about your inheritance, Horace and I will arrive by jet and call them liars to their faces."

"I wonder—would you and Mr. Brown write out a statement of what you know about Prescott, the time of his disappearance, and what you saw and heard later at the house, and have it notarized or witnessed or something and send it to me as quickly as possible?"

"Of course we will, this very afternoon, and it will be in the mail before night. And if you need us, we'll come."

"I wouldn't dream of it."

"Well, to tell the truth, playing golf and bridge and lolling around just doesn't keep us occupied enough. My daughter couldn't be nicer or make us more welcome, but we haven't anything useful to do."

"I'll call you if I need you."

"I'll tell you what we can do," Mrs. Brown said. "I'm a camera enthusiast and I have pictures of your father and mother, and a couple of shots I made of your grandmother; one of them is posed beside a tintype of her mother. Just for fun and contrast, you know. I don't know how clearly they'd come out, but they should provide plenty of evidence that they were not institutionalized, if any idiot dares to say a

140

word. I'll get copies off to you—I have my own darkroom
—and you should have them within a week."

"You're wonderful," I assured her.

I put down the phone and sat staring at it. The most
stunning revelation was that Terry had known from the
beginning that Prescott had disappeared. She had assured
the Browns that he had gone on to bigger and better things.
Had she put their address in her private file so that it would
not be found? Did she know that Prescott had lain in that
shallow grave behind the house? Did she know who had put
him there and why he had been shot? Was she responsible
for the condition in which I had found the house? Without
Dale's intervention I would have had to abandon the place.

But Terry could not have done it single-handed. Terry
could not have tampered with the brakes. She could not have
mugged me. She could not have opened that window in the
night to shake my confidence in my sanity and drive me back
to New York and Gerald's protection.

I needed time to sort things out. Of one thing I was now
assured. There was no insanity in my mother's family. Then
why had Gerald told Hazel such a whopping lie, such a cruel
lie?

Gerald—Terry—Sam. All right, there was a logical link,
but for the life of me I couldn't figure out any conceivable
motive. All my life Gerald had been my best friend. No,
whatever was at stake, Gerald had no part in it.

I helped Hazel hang the first-floor curtains, agreed that the
whole house was lighter and brighter and gayer and then
went up to my own room saying I needed to catch up on
some sleep. I needed someone to talk to, but not Hazel;
someone like Donald Gregory with his quick understanding
and ready sympathy.

In my large shoulderbag I found a little paperbook volume

141

of verse and I curled up on the chaise longue with Mother's mink lap robe over my knees, and opened the book at randon.

Fear in a handful of dust. Perhaps it was apropos, but I was in no mood for T. S. Eliot's pessimism. *Unto the breach, dear friends.* Henry V's rallying call had always reminded me of a football coach encouraging his men, a warlike hero with the mind of a boy scout. I flipped more pages.

Why, I wondered irritably, did Dale have to take himself off at the very moment when I needed to consult with him? A whole new situation had been uncovered and there was no one with whom to discuss it. What was I supposed to do: *Wait upon the hour and time of your desire?* Hey, this won't do. Dale had headed as fast as he could go to his loving Isabelle. A married woman, too, one who had changed her mind and would do anything he wanted. The hell with Isabelle! I slammed shut the book.

The sound was echoed from outside as a car door slammed. Perhaps, after all, Donald had come to pay another call. I heard Hazel open the door and exclaim and I slipped off my robe and into a soft leaf-green dress. I noticed that the bruises on my throat were fading, but I tucked a silk scarf into the neck of my dress to conceal them.

When I reached the living room, it was not Donald Gregory; it was Gerald Stephens who awaited me. He gave me a quick searching look and then he held out his arms and I walked into them and rested my head for a moment against his shoulder. Gerald was still the same! That was the best thing that had happened since I had reached this house.

"You'll spend the night, of course," I said. "There's an extra bedroom and we'd love to have you."

"I hoped you'd ask me."

"As though that were necessary! Tell Sam to bring in your suitcase. He can have one of the beds over the garage. Dale

142

has gone to the city for a few days, so he can have the place to himself."

"I drove up alone. Sam hasn't had a vacation in a long time and he wanted a few days off. As there is nothing pressing at the moment, nothing Terry can't handle, I decided to give myself a holiday."

"I'll make up the bed," Hazel said. "It's lovely to have you, Gerald."

When she had gone, Gerald gave me that intent, searching look again and I said impulsively, without having intended to, "Gerald, why did you tell Hazel that I have a streak of madness in me, inherited insanity from my mother and her mother and her mother? Three generations. And that Father let them both die to prevent Mother from being institutionalized?"

Gerald stared at me, his mouth opening and closing like a drowning fish. "My God!" he said at length. "My God!" He fumbled for a cigarette and lighted it, his hand shaking. I got up to move an ashtray closer to him.

He was white with shock. I heard the tall clock in the hall bong the half hour. Early for cocktails, but he needed a stimulant. I went out to mix cocktails and came back with mixing pitcher and glasses. I poured him a drink.

"Exactly what did Hazel tell you?" he asked, after sampling the drink and deciding that it was to his liking.

"Just what I told you."

"When was this?"

"The night I reached New York."

"I wouldn't have believed she was capable of such a thing."

"Why not, if she believed it to be true?"

"But, good God, there's not a word of truth in it! Your mother was as sane as anyone I ever knew; a touch of Bismarck about her, but that was only tiresome and exhausting,

143

it wasn't psychotic. And your father was incapable of violence in any form and, frankly, he was incapable of any decisive action where your mother was concerned. He disliked emotional tension; he simply gave in."

"But then why—?" I was bewildered.

"That," Gerald said grimly, "is what we are going to find out."

As though on cue, Hazel came bustling in, her face alight with good will, and said, "Your room is all ready for you, Gerald."

She added, and I suppose she honestly couldn't help it, "I put an extra blanket and an eiderdown beside the bed in case you should need them; that is, if Maggie does one of her crazy tricks and leaves a window wide open on the freezing air."

"Crazy tricks?" Gerald said softly.

"Well—"

"When," he asked, "did I ever tell you that Maggie had inherited insanity and that her father committed murder and suicide?"

"Why you never did," she said indignantly.

"Hazel, you told me the whole story," I protested.

"But I didn't say Gerald told me; I just said that he knew."

"And what made you think I knew?" he asked.

"Terry told me so."

FOURTEEN

When Hazel, with obvious reluctance, had left us and gone up to bed, Gerald threw another log on the fire, mixed himself a light nightcap, and said, his voice sounding spent with emotional strain, "Well, we've got to face it, Maggie; your trustee seems to have put his faith in some very strange characters. Whether it's galloping senility or just plain stupidity, I trusted Terry completely. I gambled on Sam and never for a moment had any reason to doubt him. Are you tired? If you aren't, I'd like to thrash this out and see what we can come up with."

So we discussed it from every angle we could think of and became more and more thoroughly confused.

"Wait," Gerald said at last, "let's get some order into this. We'll start with Hazel. I don't hold any brief for Hazel, but I honestly think she is truthful; that is, as far as she recognizes truth when she sees it. She began to press you to come home for the simple reason that she was going to lose her job and she wanted you to take care of her. Not that she admitted that to herself. She persuaded herself that you needed her. All evening she's been hovering over you to prove to me how essential she is to you.

145

"Well, then, when she has broken you down and you decide to come home, she fastens on me to be sure to be in a position to force your hand. And that is where Terry comes in. Terry usually dines with me once a week, and that is when she found out in consternation that you were not only coming home but you planned to return to your own house. She made up that story of the inherited insanity for Hazel's benefit to prevent you from going off on your own. It's obvious now that she deliberately concealed the Browns' address so you could not reach them, as she had suppressed from me their report on the activities in this house."

He paused for a moment, running one thin hand through his hair. "So far so good. When you were determined to come up here, she got Sam to try to kill you and, when that failed, to make your car unsafe. And when everything failed, to see that this house was uninhabitable."

I had never seen him look so tired, or so at a loss. His loss of faith in two trusted people had made him unsure of himself.

"After all," I said, "we don't have any proof of any of this. It's all speculation."

"Not the house or the car; not Prescott's murder or the Browns' report that never reached me. The core of the whole matter seems to lie in the use to which this house has been put by Terry for the past two years, or perhaps even before when Prescott stumbled on the truth. And this attempt to make you think you have inherited insanity. Of all the damnable—"

I told him then about the open window, intended to convince me I had done it myself. And it was Terry who had told me to meet him at the Pierre.

"But I distinctly told her the Plaza," he said. "Anyhow she knows I lunch there several times a week."

After a few moments he set down his empty glass. When

146

I reached out to refill it, he shook his head. "I don't want escape," he said; "I want some facts."

"The only fact is Prescott's murder." The rest—the lights, the cars that used the garage, the telephone calls—there seemed to be nothing to go on. Everything had stopped when I arrived, including the telephone calls when Mr. Gregory arranged to have the number changed.

"Which reminds me, what sort of fellow is this Gregory? Terry assured me he was all right, but by now—" Gerald made a helpless gesture.

"He's delightful and cultivated. He came to our rescue that first night after we landed in the snowbank and couldn't have been more helpful. Even Hazel thinks he is charming, though she distrusts his man Philippe and attributes all kinds of sinister motives to him, but you know Hazel."

"I'm beginning to wonder if I know anyone. Except you, Maggie. Thank God, you are always the same." When I made no reply, he went on heavily, "At least I am glad you have someone to call on in case of need."

"Well, actually, Donald is crippled and just out of the hospital, and his man Philippe is sullen and grudging about everything he does. But human." I laughed and described my accidental peeping Tom act when Philippe was holding a woman in a passionate embrace.

"Donald was amused when I told him and, I suspect, relieved, as the situation is apt to ensure his keeping Philippe with him until he is stronger."

"And this fellow you picked up at a garage. Terry told me—" He checked himself and made a fumbling gesture.

"Terry came up like a bat out of hell and did her best to get Dale out of here."

"She seemed to think that he had managed to ingratiate himself with you and got on the most familiar terms in an astonishingly short time."

147

"We were having a drink when she arrived. Dale isn't a garage mechanic. He's a Harvard graduate and a man of cultivation and breeding. Without his help we'd have had to go back to New York. Both Hazel and I feel that we owe him a lot."

"A man with such qualifications working in a garage?"

"I don't really know just what he is doing," I said bluntly. "I'm fairly sure he was staying at the garage in order to keep an eye on this house. After all, it's a dead end and he had a vantage point from which to observe any cars coming this way. He's up to something, but all I can feel reasonably sure of is that he's on the side of the angels."

Gerald made a slight grimace but no comment, his eyes intent on my face.

"I'm fairly sure he recognized the hunter—if he was a hunter—who, I realize now, was looking for that grave. And I saw him give a message to a young man passing this house who was pretending to be a skier. And he tangled with whoever it was who opened the window the second time."

I broke off. "Oh, I know it sounds like cops and robbers."

"It sounds a great deal worse than that. But you trust him, don't you? You—like him."

"Yes," I said, "I like him. The hell of it is that I don't know whether or not I trust him."

And tonight, I thought, he is with his Isabelle, who is willing to capitulate and do whatever he likes.

"Well," Gerald sounded unutterably tired, "that seems to be that. We have covered everything, haven't we?"

As I got up to go to bed, Gerald asked abruptly, "What happened to the gun this Dale claims he took from the unknown intruder?"

"He left it with me when he went to New York."

"I'd like to check on it if you don't mind."

My hesitation lasted only a moment. "Of course." I un-

148

locked a drawer in the pretty inlaid desk in the living room and handed it to him gingerly. "It's loaded."

He made sure the catch was on and slipped it in his pocket. "We'll see what the police can find out about this. I think I'll have a talk with your state troopers in the morning, if that's all right with you."

"Of course it's all right. Gerald, you look tired to death."

"I am getting to be an old man, you know." He spoke with an undercurrent of bitterness.

"Nonsense. Don't make such a blatant plea for sympathy." I laughed and kissed his cheek. "I hope you'll find everything you need in your room. Sorry I haven't a thing for you to read."

He smiled. "How about the binoculars? There's nothing like being a peeping Tom, I've been told. My life seems to have been devoid of so many harmless amusements."

When I tapped lightly on his door, he opened it, wearing a warm dressing gown. He chuckled when I handed him the binoculars. I whispered, "Have fun."

II

Next morning Gerald slept late. Hazel was in a mood of unaccustomed sullenness and she did not try to hide her grievance.

"I must say, Maggie, I don't see why you talked about me that way to Gerald. As though I'd made up lies about him."

"I guess I misunderstood you, Hazel, when you told me he knew about the insanity. I didn't understand you'd got all that from Terry."

"Then it isn't true?"

"Not a word of it," I said cheerfully. I told her about my calls to the MacTavishes and the Browns. "There was nothing wrong with Mother or her mother or her mother."

"Well, I must say that's a great relief. You can't help

149

feeling uneasy when you're with someone—unpredictable."
Hazel put a slice of ham on my plate and a fried egg and some
hashed browned potatoes.

"What on earth is all this?"

"I fixed a hearty breakfast because I thought Gerald would
enjoy it, but there's no point in waiting. It will just spoil. I'll
cook him another breakfast when he comes down."

"Sorry to make you all this work."

"Oh, it isn't the work. I like cooking. It's just—well, being
left out of things."

"Gerald and I had a lot of private matters to discuss last
night, Hazel."

"I can't imagine what you'd have to say that was a secret."

I didn't enlighten her and she went on worrying it. "What
do you think made Terry tell me those lies about you?"

"I don't know any more about it than you do. What I
suspect is that she wanted you to prevent me from coming
up here and, if I did, to convince you that any ideas I might
have were irrational. I think she and Sam arranged that
mugging and the work on the brakes and what was done to
this house."

Hazel chewed rhythmically, rather like a cow, the same
ruminative expression on her face. Then she said abruptly,
"But they couldn't, either of them, have opened the window!
They weren't here."

"I know. It always comes back to that."

When Gerald finally emerged from his room, there were
new lines in his face, which was a curious gray color. His
eyes were sunken. Obviously he hadn't slept. He refused
Hazel's offer of breakfast but drank two cups of black
coffee.

Afterwards he came down with his suitcase and I gave a
little exclamation of distress and protest.

150

"I'll have to get back." He patted the pocket in which he had stowed the revolver. "I'll check on this. I want to have a talk with your state police and I'll call on your tenant to thank him for his kindness to you. That was a wonderful dinner, Hazel. Maggie, my dear, take care of yourself. I wish to God you'd go back with me but," as he saw the mute protest on my lips, "I won't press it." He kissed my cheek lightly and went out to his car.

While Hazel did the dishes, I went up to strip Gerald's bed. The binoculars were on the windowsill and it occurred to me, with something of a shock, that he had actually used them during the night. Somehow the idea of Gerald taking pleasure in voyeurism was hard to accept.

Poor Gerald! He was going back to deal with the treachery of the two people he had most trusted: Terry and Sam. Going back, too, with the knowledge that it would never be of any avail to renew his proposal to me.

Which brought me to Dale and the revolver Gerald had taken with him. At least Gerald would settle one question that tormented me: was it Dale's revolver or did it belong to the intruder who had disappeared in the night? An intruder without a car, who could not have gone far in the cold. An intruder who had no existence.

Anything, I told myself not quite truthfully, is better than not knowing.

I took the binoculars up to their attic resting place to escape Hazel's questions, turned them idly on Donald's house, where I saw Gerald's limousine parked in front. He had meant it about calling on my tenant to thank him. Gerald's kindness to me was beyond words and I had, as Terry pointed out, made small return.

I crossed the room to the small window on the other side and caught my breath in sheer delight. Two deer were grazing peacefully on the bark of young trees. I knew in time they would destroy the trees, but at the moment they were a joy to watch. Then with a flurry and a flash of white tails they bounded away out of sight. Something had alarmed them.

He came slowly through the woods, walking on snowshoes, bundled up as though for the arctic, a camera slung around his neck. There was something familiar about the man and I realized it was his air of general ineptitude on the snowshoes. I recognized him then. This was the non-skier to whom Dale had tossed the box of cigarettes.

He glanced casually toward the house where Hazel was crashing around in the kitchen. Then he pulled something out of his pocket and hurled it up onto the little porch that ran around all four sides of the garage apartment. After waiting for a few minutes, he turned and plodded awkwardly back through the woods.

I hauled on heavy slacks and boots, pulled a lined jacket over my sweater, a cap over my head, and went out, closing the front door quietly so as not to alert Hazel's attention. Passing the kitchen window was tricky and I crouched down. Then the telephone rang and Hazel went to answer it. I went past the kitchen like a shot, raced up the steps to the apartment and picked up the weighted cigarette box that the stranger had thrown there.

I had to go back through the front door, as the back one was bolted from the inside now that Dale was gone. I heard Hazel say, "I don't know. I called her and she didn't answer. I can't imagine—oh, here she is! What on earth were you doing outside?"

"Freezing. That's why I decided not to take a walk."

"Well, Terry is on the phone. Something has come up and she wants to ask Gerald's advice." She handed me the phone

152

though she could have given the answer herself.

"Terry?" I couldn't help the coldness in my voice. "Gerald just stayed overnight. He will be back in New York some time today. If that's all—" Without waiting for a reply, I broke the connection.

In my room I stood for some time juggling the cigarette box from one hand to the other. It wasn't my property. I had no right to open it. On the other hand, what went on at this house concerned me deeply and I had every right. My scruples went down like ninepins. I opened the box. There was a thin stone to weigh it down and wrapped around the stone a sheet of paper with a typed message:

Followed P. to the Buckeye Tavern last night and got him drunk. Very cagey. Hates the fuzz. Served time or I'm cockeyed.

After fourth drink—mine went into a convenient if unexpected cuspidor nearby—I flashed that billfold you provided with a nice view of a flock of fifties. Shot in the dark. Dropped the idea I'd just got paid for passing H. Now my distributor had been picked up and I was hounded by customers going nuts. He made no direct response.

I'd give a leg to get into that place. As you failed with the garage apartment, he must have it cached in the house. How he manages without G finding out, I don't know. The poor guy is probably too much of an invalid to notice. I expect that's why P. took the job. A break for him. I hope you clear up the N.Y. end. I have a hunch something is ready to break.

P. and I are to meet tomorrow. He had a lot of

153

personal questions, drunk as he was, but, thanks to your drill, I had answers to all of them. Did he believe me? God knows. The chief problem is that if he's suspicious, he may set up an appointment where I can't get reinforcements. Chris.

FIFTEEN

Hazel, who had settled down before a crackling fire with one of her romances, her transistor radio at her side throbbing out old musical comedy tunes, got up when she heard a car pass and went to the window. "That's the second time a police car has gone by. They must be patrolling this road."

So Gerald had paid his promised visit to the state police. Not long after that, he called from New York, his voice still betraying his exhaustion.

"Maggie? I thought you'd better know that the gun is registered to Philippe Thibault."

"Philippe!" I was startled. But of course it made sense. Only someone who had a shelter close by could have worked that stunt with the window, which meant that Dale had told me the truth about the intruder.

"So we have a link now," Gerald went on; "Terry to Sam to this Philippe who works for Gregory. The state police are looking into the Frenchman's background and don't want to show their hand until they have something concrete."

"But shouldn't Donald know? He's in no condition to protect himself."

Gerald hesitated. "I suppose someone should tip him off.

155

But the police want a case before they move. If you were to call him, the call might be overheard by Philippe."

"I'll ask him to have dinner here tomorrow," I decided. "I can let him know how much we've found out—"

"Remember that all we actually know is that the gun your man took away from an unidentified intruder was registered to Philippe."

"I suppose you know that Terry called here because there was something she couldn't handle and I told her you'd be back today."

"Terry is not in the office. She hasn't been here all day."

"What do you think happened to her?"

"Oh, I know where she is; at least where she was." Gerald broke off and then said in a different tone, "Oh, there you are, Terry. Take care of yourself, Maggie. Keep in touch."

I called Donald, who answered the telephone himself and accepted with alacrity my dinner invitation. Hazel, overhearing the conversation, rushed out into the hall as soon as I had finished.

"We've got to have more food. With this thaw, driving will be no problem. I'm going to the village to get some supplies if that's all right with you. Heaven knows whether the roads will be open tomorrow, and anyhow I need time to plan a proper meal."

"Fine." I went to get money out of my handbag.

"I think I'll get a turkey," Hazel decided. "And some chestnuts for the stuffing." She began to make a list. "Cranberry sauce. Do you think he'd prefer sweets to whipped potatoes? Some of those rolls you just brown and serve." She was happy as could be.

"And a good dry white wine for dinner," I said firmly. She was too happy to be preparing a dinner for Donald to be as obstinate as usual.

When she had gone in the Gremlin, driving slowly and

156

gripping the wheel hard, I realized that it was the first time I had been alone in the house. I wandered aimlessly from room to room, looked out to see the icicles dripping from the roof as the sun caught them, and hear the soft plop as snow slid off the roof onto the ground. The sky was a blazing blue.

I bundled into ski pants and boots, two sweaters and a thick jacket, pulled a wool cap over my head, and went out. The air was cold but it felt sweet and clean. I walked to the top of the road with its narrow turnaround and then went on into the woods. I had started with the belief that I was going to try to sort out my thoughts, unscramble the things that had happened in the past few days, discover if I could what roles Philippe and Terry and Sam—and Dale—were playing in the game going on around me. But what I really wondered was what side Dale was on? Not Philippe's. That was all I could be sure of, to judge by the message in the cigarette box.

The short twilight of February came almost unnoticed until I nearly ran into a tree and discovered how swiftly darkness had fallen. I turned back, not in panic, because I had known these woods all my life, and there was one huge double maple that provided a landmark and a guide. Keeping that on my left, I went as swiftly as I could back to the road. The maple finally blended into the darkness and I did have a moment of uneasiness until I saw a faint glimmer of light. As I went around a mound of snow into which I nearly floundered, I saw the blinking lights and hurried toward them.

Dale was standing beside his motorcycle. I'd never been so glad to see anyone in my life, but there was no reason to believe he shared my feeling.

"Just what the hell do you think you are doing?" he demanded. "The temperature is dropping fast, it's below freezing and it's pitch dark. You don't know who you might run into in the woods." He seemed unreasonably angry.

157

"All I was afraid of was that I wouldn't run into anyone."

He pulled off his glove and touched my cold cheek. "Fool girl!"

"When did you get back? Oh, Dale, I have so much to tell you."

"All in good time. I've picked up a few items myself. Get on back."

"What?"

"This," he said with elaborate carefulness, "is a motorcycle. This is where I sit. That is where you sit."

"But—"

"Don't be such a sissy. Nothing to it. You just hang onto me."

"But I don't need a ride to get home. I can see the porch light from here. I left it on for Hazel, who went to the village to shop."

"We aren't going home," he told me coolly, picked me up and put me on the back seat. "Now," as he got on, "you put your arms around me. Just hang on, that's all you have to do. You might even find it a pleasant habit to get into."

At my outraged expression he grinned, the motor started with its usual horrible explosions and we were off. I hung on. The last thing I'd ever expected was that at any time in my life I'd be one of those females who cling to the drivers of motorcycles. Afterwards Dale assured me that we hadn't gone more than thirty miles an hour at any time, but it seemed like eighty to me. I couldn't speak or protest. I kept my face as close to his coat as possible because of the wind that blew my protesting words against my mouth. As we roared through the village, we passed Hazel, who was driving the Gremlin sedately home. Thank God she didn't see me. I tugged at Dale's coat and shouted, but the words blew away.

158

When he stopped, it was at a small and rather dingy tavern. He lifted me off the motorcycle.

"We aren't going in there!" I said incredulously.

"Perfectly respectable. I know it looks like a pirate's hideout, but it's a family-owned business. No drunkenness allowed. No noisy parties. No funny business. You'll see why when you meet the boss."

"But I can't go in like this." My cap had blown off in the first mile. My hair had slipped out of the roll on the back of my neck, which was the only way I could control it. At the moment it covered me like a cloud, concealing my face, hanging to my hips. It was a bird's nest. My nose was red and shiny and my eyes watery.

"Come on." Dale took my arm. "It's dark in there anyhow and nobody will notice."

The tavern, which looked vaguely disreputable from the outside, was unexpectedly cheerful inside, with a crackling fire in the grate. There was no one in the booths and only one customer at the bar, chatting with the owner. He must have been about six feet seven and weighed three hundred pounds, all muscle. I could understand now why the tavern was run along peaceable lines.

"Luigi," Dale said in a low tone, "was Prescott's closest friend. It was in this tavern that he spent his Saturday evenings. Luigi feels strongly about his death. Under that placid exterior there is a volcano just waiting to go up."

The customer at the bar was making a mug of beer last as long as he could. He glanced around casually as we came in and then he stared. Well, I couldn't blame him. I did my best to brush my hair off my face and out of my eyes. It was so tangled I could not even braid it.

Dale spoke to the big bartender, whom he seemed to know, said good evening to the customer, and came to lead

159

me to one of the booths.

"Don't do that," he said, watching my struggle with my hair. "Let it alone. It's beautiful."

"I didn't know you'd be back today," I said.

"I got through my business more quickly than I expected."

"With Isabelle?" I could have bitten off my tongue.

"No," he said coolly, "but I think the end of that job is in sight. With a little bit of luck. By the way, she wants to know you."

"She—"

"My sister. I tried to give her a vague idea but she thought I was delirious and I hadn't even seen your hair then."

I could feel the color flooding my cheeks. And I could feel the delight that seemed to pervade my whole body. His sister. And he wanted her to know me.

I tried to sound as casual as possible. "You missed a caller today."

"Oh?" He was amused at my inept attempt to change the subject.

I handed him the cigarette box. In a burst of honesty I said, "I opened it."

His lips twitched. "Not the first time, is it?"

"I didn't open that letter," I protested. "I—just held it up to the light."

Dale leaned back and shouted with laughter and after a moment of embarrassment I joined in. If confession is good for the soul, then my soul was in pristine condition, but I realized that he had suspected it all the time.

Before he could open the box, the huge bartender came over with two napkin-wrapped tall glasses.

"Careful," Dale warned me. "That's scalding."

"What is it?"

160

"Hot rum punch, and if you've never tasted it, you have an experience awaiting you."

The steam from the glass was fragrant with rum and cinnamon and a number of spices, and when I took a cautious sip, almost blistering my lips, I gave a long sigh. "It's wonderful."

"Guaranteed to warm you up," Dale said cheerfully. While I experimented with the hot rum punch, Dale opened the cigarette box and read the note. When he spoke, he took me completely by surprise, a situation to which I should have become accustomed. "Wouldn't you like to ask the delightful Mr. Gregory to dine with you tomorrow?"

"I already have," I told him, "and he accepted."

Dale stood up, leaned across the table, and kissed me on both cheeks. "A medal for Maggie," he said. Then he slid out from his side of the booth and went along the bar to where the one customer still worked on his mug of beer. He spoke a few words and then came back to me. He didn't explain, but by that time I didn't expect him to. It was I who rushed into explanations.

I told him about Gerald's visit, about how Terry had lied to Hazel about the inherited insanity, confirmed by my calls to the MacTavishes and the Browns, and how Gerald and I had figured that Terry and Sam, working together, had arranged to keep me away from the house.

Dale started to speak, checked himself, and began to work on his drink, stirring it with a long stick of cinnamon so that the fumes wafted across the table, practically making me drool. There are drinks and drinks and, though I am no authority, I knew this was the very king of drinks for a cold night. It warmed the heart as well as the body.

"So I gave Gerald the gun you left with me and he checked

161

it with the state police. It was registered to Philippe Thibault, Donald's man."

"I couldn't be less surprised," Dale said, deflating my excitement, when I had expected him to jump up and down. No doubt about it, Dale was an exasperating man. "After all, use the head, Maggie. That's what it's for, not just to grow that beautiful hair. No one could travel far on such a night, without transportation, to pull a stunt like that opened window. It had to be either Philippe or his boss."

"Well, it couldn't have been Donald. The man is lame and frail and anyhow he's too—"

"Devastatingly attractive," Dale concluded.

"Well, he is," I retorted. "Anyhow I thought he ought to be warned about Philippe, so that's why I asked him to dinner tomorrow. Hazel is going to kill the fatted calf, turkey and white wine, and I'm going to break the bad news."

"In normal circumstances I'd put my foot down about that," Dale said, "but it seems to be a bonus right now."

"Dale," and I was deadly serious now, "what is all this about? You're mixed up in it, aren't you?"

"I know about it."

"How deeply are you involved?"

"Until it is cleared up, one way or the other, I'm in it right up to the eyebrows."

I'd been sipping at my drink and now I pushed it aside. It was only tepid now and it had lost its magic. As Dale was about to signal for a refill, I shook my head.

"I've got to know, Dale. Who are you? What are you?" When he made no reply, I said, "Why did you go to New York?"

He too pushed away his unfinished drink and offered me a cigarette, which I refused. He lighted his own, taking his time. The other customer had left the bar and drifted out of

162

the tavern, and the huge bartender, after raising his eyebrows at Dale and getting a shake of the head, had gone through a swinging door into a kitchen, brightly lighted and spotless. I caught a glimpse of a red-checked tablecloth and a woman ladling spaghetti from a boiling kettle and heaping it on a plate.

"I didn't go to New York to see Isabelle," Dale said, implying that he knew that was what I most wanted to know, "though I spent the night at her house. Since her husband's suicide, she's been as lost as though she were alone on a raft at sea. They were terribly in love. Later, when you know each other, perhaps you can help her break out of the shell she's built around her. But first I'll answer your last question. I went to New York to have a long heart-to-heart talk with Mr. Stephens's trusted chauffeur, Sam Stokes."

After a moment he said, consideringly, "You do look silly with your mouth hanging open."

I closed it, opened it again. "But why Sam?"

"Because he's a cagey devil and all attempts to get something out of him by telephone had failed. Or so I thought. But I'd misjudged him. He'd taken a few days' leave and he got himself a job in Stephens's warehouse as a night watchman. We—some friends and I—arranged for the regular man to go to Chicago to see a sick mother. When he comes back, he's in for a spot of trouble. More trouble than he ever dreamed of."

"It would help if I knew what you were talking about."

"This whole business is concerned with the distribution of heroin. And it struck me that a big importing business would be a natural for getting the stuff into the country. And my hunch paid off. A lovely link from Philippe Thibault's uncle in Marseilles to Stephens's warehouse to your house, where contacts were made with the distributors who used the code word Cincinnati. It makes my blood run cold, Maggie, to think of what might have happened when you walked straight into the situation."

It was a long time before I said numbly, "Gerald's business. Gerald! All the time."

SIXTEEN

With a startled exclamation Dale slid out of the booth and fumbled in his pockets. "Have you any change?"

"I just went out for a walk."

"Luigi will trust me for a few coins."

"What's wrong?"

"It's after six o'clock, woman, and Hazel will probably call the state police when she doesn't find you at home. And that is the last thing wanted at this time."

He went through the swinging door so fast it swung wide behind him and in a few minutes he came back to drop coins in the public telephone on the wall.

"This is Dale," he said. He listened, trying in vain to interrupt a flood of speech. At last he said, "It's quite all right. She's with me. I got back early and drove her to the village. When I realized how worried you might be, I decided to call you at once." Apparently he managed to sooth Hazel. "Well, I don't know exactly. We'll have something to eat here. Keep the porch light on, will you? Thanks so much."

He came back, mopping his head. "That was a narrow shave. She was just on the verge of calling the state troopers. I told her—but you heard that."

"But, Dale, we can't eat here."

"Don't be a snob, darling. The place is neat but not gaudy. The kitchen is spotless. This has been my home away from home for some weeks."

"Well, at least you seem to have been adequately nourished," I commented. "I never took much stock in that pitiful tale of making stew out of practically nothing."

He grinned. "Don't be like that, Maggie."

I shook my head. "Keep your cajolery for Hazel. Dale, I've got to know. Who are you?"

He knew as well as I did why it was important to me. He waited until bowls of minestrone had been set before us and the monstrous Luigi, whose muscles bulged forbiddingly and whose expression was mild as milk, had gone back through the swinging door.

He watched me taste the soup and nodded agreement. It was excellent.

"My name is Dale Armstrong Curtis. I was born in nineteen forty-five in an old house on Beacon Street in Boston. I have one younger sister, Isabelle, who, after her marriage, became one of the jet set, London for first nights, parties on the Riviera, skiing at St. Moritz. My father was a judge who has since reluctantly retired and now writes books on the improvements needed in the speedy administration of the law. My mother, if she had had less money, would have been a contented housewife. Instead she is a devoted bridge player now that she's grown too old for tennis. She still plays a good game of golf and she'd rather be seen dead than in one of those electric golf carts. She can do her own walking, thank God! She sponsors promising young musicians with the touching belief that she is a thwarted pianist, which is an error of judgment on her part. But if you ever laugh when she plays for you, which she will, I'll strangle you with these

166

two hands. If you don't mind puns, you should like her a lot. She's as much fun as anyone I know."

Dale devoted himself to soup. When Luigi had brought heaping plates of spaghetti and a crisp salad, Dale sprinkled cheese on his spaghetti and cocked an eyebrow at me. "Do you want any more of this entrancing autobiography?"

"You haven't really told me anything yet, have you? About yourself, I mean."

"If you are asking about my profession, I'm a political cartoonist. I sign my stuff Vox Populi."

Of all things that was the last I would have expected. I'd been seeing those cartoons for nearly five years. They had twice won awards. Three collections of them had been published in book form and I owned all three. In his own field Dale sat unchallenged at the top.

"You?"

"Even I. With my little drawing pencil. The advantage of a job like mine is that, as long as I get my stuff in on time, I don't always have to hang around New York. An advantage in a case like this, of course."

For a little while we ate spaghetti, Dale rolling his expertly on fork and spoon while I managed to cut up small enough bits to be manageable without dribbling. I gave up halfway through, but Dale cleared his plate. When the roast chicken came, I could only nibble at it, but his appetite seemed to be undiminished.

"There's a lot of me to feed," he said apologetically.

To Luigi's concern we refused spumoni for dessert but accepted coffee. Luigi said something to Dale in Italian and Dale grinned. Afterwards he explained solemnly that Luigi had commiserated with him on having a girl with so little appetite. A man wanted a nice cozy armful. He gave me a challenging look to which I did not respond. I had learned

167

smatterings of half a dozen languages during my three years abroad. Luigi had actually said, "The woman was there all night. She left this morning. Giuseppe saw her drive past the garage."

"So you are Vox Populi."

Dale pushed aside his coffee cup and pulled a notebook and pencil out of his pocket and sketched rapidly. He tore out the sheet and handed it to me. It was a wicked sketch of Hazel sitting at a ouija board with a witch on a broomstick hovering over her. Then he did one of me striding along the road, "as though the hounds of hell were after you," he said. Seen from the back, I was recognizable only by my clothes.

"That's cheating," I protested. "You didn't show my face."

"I'll do that some other time." He did one of Sam with his sidelong look and bland face.

I put out a hand to stop him. "Dale, I've got to know about Gerald and the heroin."

Instead he went on drawing. This time he took longer and there were two heads on the page. One was Terry full face, with that short cropped hairdo and her thick glasses. The other was in profile, an unexpectedly lovely profile and heavy-lidded eyes without glasses. Glamorous. Voluptuous.

"Terry?" I said, stunned. "Terry?" Then I gasped. "When I looked out of the window, it was Terry I saw with Philippe." I shook my head. "This seems to be more than I can digest at one time. Terry and Philippe. Philippe! So that's why he said, 'How in hell did you get here?' when Hazel and I came banging at his door. It must have been quite a shock. I remember being puzzled when he opened the door on a chain. Very cautious. I suppose, if he was involved in something illegal, he had to be careful. But what is your interest in all this?"

"My sister. Or rather her husband. Bill was one of the

most charming guys I've ever met, gay, fun-loving, the reckless kind who wants to try anything. Well, he smoked a couple of marijuana cigarettes and liked the feeling of irresponsibility they gave him. Isabelle didn't approve of it but he laughed. So he tried heroin and he got hooked. He tried to kick the habit but he wasn't a strong guy, just a nice one, and when he realized what he was doing to himself and to Isabelle, he just swam out to sea one morning from a little place they had near Greenwich where they belonged to the yacht club and spent a couple of months every year.

"Isabelle didn't go into a flap or have hysterics or even cry. She just withdrew. You can't reach her at all. She wouldn't even talk about it. Well, I worked on her for weeks and finally she capitulated and said she would give me all the information she had and all the hints she had been able to gather about where and how Bill had got the stuff. It was tough for her because she wanted to put the whole thing behind her but, of course, no one can do that."

Dale had pointed out that she could help prevent other people being victimized in the same way and he set out to run down the people who had provided Bill with heroin and put them behind bars.

"One thing Isabelle has plenty of is money, and I make a nice hunk of change, so we had all the cash we needed."

It had taken months of patient work and false trails to piece together fragmentary information and to trace the distribution point to my house. That was when Dale arranged with the garage owner to stake out there because it made a perfect observation point for the dead-end road that led to the twin houses.

"He was scared of being involved in anything, so I gave him two hundred fifty dollars a month and swore to keep him out of trouble. I'm not in this by myself, of course. Unofficially I'm giving aid and comfort to the Treasury boys. It was

169

one of them who posed as a bounty-hunter when he was actually looking for Prescott's body. And there's Chris, of course." Dale grinned. "Chris never had it so rough. He gets carried away. It was his idea to keep an eye on your house on skis that time you saw me handing him a message. And he came out on snowshoes to throw me the message," and Dale grinned wickedly at me, "that you read. He was here tonight, but I didn't introduce him because I didn't expect to unburden my soul to you this way. He's been in love with Isabelle all his life but, of course, he didn't have a chance against Bill's charm. I hope someday she'll discover just what a good guy he is.

"Oh, and then there's Luigi, who has been a tower of strength. He's all for law and order. He picks up rumors and passes them on. He's been wondering about Philippe for several years. He was always cropping up somewhere but until he landed a job with Gregory a little while ago, he seemed to have no regular occupation. And Luigi's prejudiced. His sister ran away with a Frenchman, so he distrusts them all."

I was silent for a long time, pondering. A lot of things were coming straight. A lot of them were muddled. "But who actually has been living in my house?"

"I'm fairly sure," Dale said, "it was Philippe. Terry knew about the vacant house, of course, far enough out of town to be unnoticed. Prescott was eliminated and they were all set to use it as a distribution center. Then when Terry found you were on your way back, she must have panicked. Anyhow, by a stroke of luck she got a new tenant for the twin house and moved Philippe in as male nurse, cook, and what have you. The chief stumbling block, of course, was the telephone. That was how they kept their organization informed about when the stuff was coming in. My God, the chances you took, Maggie!"

170

"Well, at least I didn't know it." I thought for a moment. "Terry and Philippe." I shook my head. "Has anyone actually been caught?"

"Well, the government boys want the big fish. They've got the names of a lot of minnows, but they haven't hauled them in yet. And they want proof. What they want is to get the big boy with the stuff in his possession."

"So that's why you searched my house so carefully the day you pretended to be looking for rats."

"That's why."

"And Donald's garage apartment?"

"Yes."

"Dale, are you planning to search Donald's house while he is having dinner with us?"

"Yes."

"What about Philippe?"

"He and Chris have set up a meeting. He'll be out of the place."

"Dale, I can't do that to Donald. It's an act of treachery. He ought to know the truth about what is going on. The whole thing."

Dale was silent.

"He isn't safe, is he?" I insisted.

"No, I don't really think he is."

"But then—"

"My brother-in-law killed himself. Other men and boys and girls and small children are taking to crime to get the money for the stuff men like Philippe and women like Terry are putting into their hands. Not personally. They leave the risks to others. One man's safety can't stand in the way of ending this thing, Maggie. You've got to understand that."

I thought it over, but I couldn't agree. To lure Donald away from his house so Dale could search it seemed a filthy trick.

171

Dale did not try to convince me. He simply waited.

"What about Sam?" I asked at length.

"Sam's okay," Dale said. "The Justice boys got him a dog trained to sniff out dope. One of them worked with him handling the dog and they went through that warehouse with a fine-tooth comb. And they hit pay dirt! You wouldn't believe the variety of ways there are of smuggling dope. It was in the frames of pictures, in the hollow corks of wine bottles, in the fake bottoms of vases. And God knows how long it's been going on. Of course the government boys fell on it with whoops of joy. They're in touch with the authorities in Marseilles who will pick up Philippe's uncle. May have done it by now. And of course the night watchman won't be seeing the world except through bars for a long, long time to come."

"Dale, how much does Gerald know about the way his importing business is being used?"

Dale gave me a sudden smile. "I doubt very much that he knows anything about it. I'm going a lot by Sam's attitude toward him. Sam would go to the stake for the guy. That's why he was persuaded to help us. No, I believe Terry got herself a job with Stephens realizing how useful a cover the importing business could be and she made herself invaluable."

"But how did the stuff get from the warehouse out to my house?"

"So far as we can figure out, the night watchman put it in cottage cheese packages which were delivered to Terry's apartment. Matter of fact, we're sure of it. It was his son who did the work for him and he told us about it quite innocently and frankly."

"His son!"

"The kid is only sixteen and he doesn't know what it's all about. Well, on weekends Terry brought the stuff up here, enjoyed a spot of love-making, and when Philippe's organization called they were told that a delivery had been made. How the stuff was repackaged and where it was picked up we don't know yet."

"Then if it wasn't Sam who tampered with the Gremlin or tried to throttle me, who was it?"

"He checked with the garage where the car was left and got hold of the night man who said he'd found a guy hovering around inside and chased him out. The description fits Philippe. And he had plenty of time to get back here before you did. You said you didn't leave until afternoon. Plenty of time. And of course Terry would have known when you'd get home from that quartet. And, if there's any question in your mind, Sam did play poker that night and he won over two hundred dollars. A memorable evening. Also," and Dale smiled again, "your trustee really was at a most important business meeting that night. Feel happier?"

I nodded. "But I knew, really I knew, that Gerald wouldn't, couldn't, hurt me."

Dale got up. "We'd better put in an appearance before Hazel calls out the National Guard." He looked at me and said quickly, "Don't look like that, darling. Nothing is going to happen to you. I swear it. Except this." He pulled me out of the booth and into his arms and kissed me. Before I could protest—and I didn't try very hard—he shouted for Luigi. This time he spoke in English. "I'm taking the lady home on the back of my motorcycle and she lost her cap."

Luigi disappeared. I heard vociferous conversation and he returned with a red wool scarf that I tied securely over my head. It was warm and smelled only slightly of garlic.

As we roared off in the night, with me hanging onto Dale, Luigi shouted a cheery good night.

173

SEVENTEEN

Hazel looked up from her novel when I came in, the red scarf tied around my head, nose and cheeks red, eyes watering.

"Where on earth could you go to eat looking like that?" she demanded. "I declare you're a perfect mess, Maggie."

"A tavern in the village. A family place and perfectly respectable. Anyhow there was no one else there."

"Well, I only hope Terry doesn't hear about you getting so intimate with a garage man."

"Oh, don't be ridiculous, Hazel. You know as well as I do that Dale is no garage man. And what we'd have done without him, I can't imagine."

"We'd have gone back to New York and taken a nice little apartment." Hazel's pet solution for her future was fast becoming a reality in her mind and something had to be done about it.

"Actually," I told her, "I haven't made any plans for the future. I may go abroad again. I know now that I'd never want to live here permanently." Remembering Prescott and the use to which the house had been put, that was true enough. "And Gerald is sure he can find a job for you in his business somewhere when you're ready to go back to work."

Hazel was silent for a long time and I felt guilty and beastly and selfish. To escape her accusing eyes and mournful mouth, I went up to bed. It was a long time before I slept. I had a lot to think about. That night I had learned too much to digest at one time: the heroin smuggling through Gerald's importing business, Terry and Philippe working together to distribute the stuff, Dale in the clear, Gerald trusting a woman who was betraying him every day of her life, Prescott shot to death by Philippe, who had tried twice to kill me to prevent my coming here, Dale's crusade to trace the heroin to its source and have the dealers imprisoned for life.

Dale was Vox Populi, a highly successful young man with an impeccable background. At least everything he had said convinced me. But of course, I admitted to myself, I had wanted to be convinced.

I spent most of the next day avoiding Hazel's reproachful eyes, rearranging furniture, mending the straps of slips and a hem that had ripped out, folding the scarf to be returned to Luigi's wife, and washing my hair, always a big job, to get the smell of garlic out of it.

Just before nightfall Dale came into the kitchen, which was redolent of the smell of roasting turkey. He saw that the dining table had been set with my best lace tablecloth, with a silver centerpiece, and the crystal and fine china that had been stored in the attic. Seeing this preparation for the reception of a single guest, Dale cocked an amused eyebrow at me.

"If you're planning to be home all evening, may I take the car?" he asked.

"Of course." I gave him the keys.

When everything was ready to serve, Hazel went upstairs to change. Once more she put on a thin silk dress, much too fancy in cut, and sprayed herself with my best perfume. It was she who ran to open the door when Philippe had guided Donald up to the porch and handed him his crutch.

Donald looked at me inquiringly. "About when?"

"As long as you like," Hazel said eagerly.

"Ten o'clock," Donald decided.

Philippe, looking sullen as usual, went back to the car. On impulse, I excused myself while Hazel fussed over Donald, and ran up to the attic. I saw the lights of the big Bentley pass Donald's house. Apparently Philippe was on his way to keep his appointment with Chris. I didn't know what the timetable was, but I hoped Philippe would be kept occupied until Dale had time to finish his search. If Philippe had one gun, he might quite likely have another, and a man who had killed once would not be likely to hesitate a second time, not with an easy fortune at stake as well as his liberty.

When I came down, Hazel, her glass of cranberry juice in her hand, was waiting patiently for me to mix the cocktails. When I had done so, Donald raised his glass in a toast and said, "You create a kind of peace around you, Maggie."

Hazel, who had been fussing restlessly with a perfectly good fire, set down the tongs, color rising in her cheeks. "If you'd seen her last night, you wouldn't have thought she was peaceful. Her hair was simply wild, riding on the back of Dale's motorcycle, looking like one of those hippies. And going to dinner with him."

Aware of the unaccustomed shrillness in her tone, Donald turned to look at her. Then he smiled. "This Dale of yours seems to be an enterprising young man. He moves in the day you meet him and now he takes you to dinner, in however unorthodox a manner. Is he joining us tonight?"

"He is not," Hazel said firmly. "When he eats here, it's in the kitchen. Though I don't say he hasn't very nice table manners."

"If he is the one equipped with a Harvard accent and a knowledge of high couture, he should do better for himself.

176

Or," and his smile broadened as he looked at me, "perhaps he couldn't do better."

"Dale is the political cartoonist who signs his stuff Vox Populi."

"The devil he is! Then why in heaven's name is he hanging around this one-horse town?"

"He doesn't have to stay in New York as long as he gets his stuff in on time."

Hazel broke in to say indignantly, "Well, I think you might have told me. I'd never have expected him to eat in the kitchen. Why, he's practically a celebrity."

Donald choked and I avoided his eyes while I refilled his glass.

"Before you have more to drink," Hazel said, as though I were practically drunk on one cocktail, "I wish you'd help me serve, Maggie."

She carved the turkey in the kitchen—"the poor man would make a mess of it in those gloves"—and I added the dressing, sweet potatoes and mashed turnips. When I had poured the water and filled the wine glasses, I called Donald, who was staring thoughtfully into the fire. He turned with a start, as though his thoughts were far away, groped for his crutch and got awkwardly to his feet. I had put him at the end of the table so he could stretch out his leg in comfort.

"But this is charming!" he exclaimed.

For a little while there was only casual conversation as we devoted ourselves to Hazel's cooking. Donald's praise brought color to her cheeks.

"If I do say so," she said complacently, "I'm a good cook. It seems to me a pity that most girls today have no idea of how to make a home for a man. Now Maggie is as helpless as a baby. If I weren't here—"

"But you're both here, for which I am heartily grateful."

177

"Well," I seized the opening, "perhaps it is just as well for you that we are here. I hate having to tell you this, Donald, but I think it is more than possible that you are or could be in danger."

The wine in his glass splashed over the edge and he mopped it up awkwardly with his napkin. "Sorry. I never get used to these gloves. I hope it won't leave a stain."

"It won't," I assured him.

"Now if it were red wine," Hazel broke in, but Donald, for the first time, interrupted her.

"What are you getting at, Maggie?"

"This Philippe of yours—"

"Well?"

"I've never trusted him for a moment," Hazel said. "And there's something familiar about him—as though I'd seen him before."

I took a long breath. "Well, I said I was going to warn you. It was a bullet from Philippe's gun that killed the caretaker Prescott two years ago."

Hazel dropped her fork with a clatter and Donald started at the sudden sound. "My dear Maggie, what on earth are you talking about? We only moved here a few days before you did and, to the best of my knowledge, Philippe doesn't own a gun."

"You moved to the twin house then but I think Philippe had been living in this house for a long time."

"And what's this about his gun?"

I explained how the window had been left open one night to make me think that I was doing odd things. So the next night Dale had decided to watch in case it happened again, struggled with a man in the dark, and got his gun. When Gerald Stephens came to see me, he turned the gun over to the police, who identified it as being registered to Philippe Thibault. "And the bullet that killed Prescott was fired from

178

that gun. So the man is a murderer. I had to tell you, to warn you."

"Well, of course, if this is true, you had to warn me. Why shouldn't you? And why is this—cartoonist—so interested in Philippe?"

I didn't know how much to tell him. I did know that Dale would have preferred me to say nothing.

"What's bothering you, Maggie?" Donald asked gently. "You really believe that Philippe is a murderer, don't you?"

"But what else can I believe?"

"But, my dear girl, if Philippe shot this caretaker of yours and buried him on your land, why on earth would he hang around this vicinity? I should think the normal thing would be to put as much distance as he could between himself and his—uh—victim."

"He couldn't go away," I explained. "He was using this house as a distribution point for heroin."

"Good God!"

I nodded. "He's been working with my trustee's assistant, Theresa Tilson, using my trustee's importing business to bring heroin from France. I realize now it was Terry I saw the other night with Philippe."

Hazel rushed into a spate of talk, exclaiming, reiterating the fact that she had never trusted Philippe and she could rely on her instincts. She was always right about people.

She broke off to remove plates, with my assistance, and to serve lime sherbet with thin cookies and coffee. No invalid should have a heavy dessert after such a dinner. Bad for his digestion, especially at night.

None of us did more than taste the sherbet, though Donald drank two cups of coffee.

"I won't put the crystal and fine china in the washer," Hazel decided. "They are much too valuable, and I'd hate to break the set. I'll wash them myself. I like to find a nice clean

179

kitchen in the morning." She added brightly, "You two go in and enjoy yourselves."

When we were in the living room, Donald said with a faint smile, "How she does enjoy being Martha! But such a dreary person in such a well-meaning way." He dismissed her then. "Maggie, where did you get hold of that fantastic story?" As I hesitated, he asked, "Was it from this cartoonist who has taken up squatters' rights in this house?"

"Yes."

"You believe him?"

My hesitation was longer this time. Then I said, "Yes."

"Not quite sure, are you? Well, I can't blame you. What's his position in all this?"

"His brother-in-law committed suicide because he got hooked on heroin. His sister almost died of grief. So Dale decided to try to find out where the heroin came from, how it was distributed, and get hold of the head man, and end at least one source of heroin to this country."

"And his investigations brought him to my Philippe! And to some woman you say works for your trustee."

"Oh, of course," I said, following my own line of thought, "it must have been Terry who suggested the open window to Philippe. She'd already done a snow job on Hazel and convinced her that I had inherited insanity."

Gerald was silent for some time, shifting the position of his lame leg as though he were in pain. His hand rested on the crutch, running up and down its length. In repose his face had a withdrawn look, the look of one who is very ill, already almost aloof from the world.

He looked up to smile at me. "I take it your enterprising friend did not want you to confide in me. Why did you?"

"But I couldn't let you take such a risk, being associated with a murderer, and not warn you. Not possibly."

180

Instinctively he stretched out his hand to me, looked at it with a grimace, and let it drop. "You're a nice girl, Maggie. A very nice girl."

"Well, after all, anyone—"

"No, not anyone. You're special with your own brand of loyalty and honesty. Which brings me—it seems to me that you are overlooking a fairly important point. And that, too, is part of your singularly trusting makeup. Your trustee. He called on me, as you probably know, apparently to find out whether I was nice for you to know." He smiled. "Or for whatever reason. In any case, he is the one who turned over the gun to the police. So far as I can make out, your cartoonist never saw the man from whom he claims to have taken it."

"But—"

"Can you honestly bring yourself to believe that a man could remain unaware for years of the fact that his importing business was being used to cover smuggling operations on a big scale? So far as I can make out, the cartoonist claims that Stephens's assistant is a prime mover, working with my Philippe. But where is the proof? What evidence links either of them to this business?"

"Dale thinks it is Philippe who tampered with my car brakes and attempted to mug me in New York."

"Philippe! But he hasn't been away from me overnight since I hired him."

"Would you know, Donald? You say you go to bed early. And you never knew when he smuggled Terry into the house."

Hazel bustled in, carrying the silver centerpiece. "I'm going to put this and the crystal back in the attic." Tonight she was hell-bent on showing Donald she was a drudge.

"If it was this Terry," Donald said when she had trudged up the stairs.

181

"Dale did a sketch of her. It was like the woman I saw with Philippe."

"Dale again." Donald looked up startled as the clock in the hall struck the half hour. "What's happened to Philippe? He was to call for me at ten and he is always prompt."

Hazel came rushing down from the attic. "Maggie, I found some binoculars in the attic and I picked them up. All the lights are on at Donald's house and there are three cars. Something must be wrong. One of them is a police car."

In the distance I heard the sound of a dog barking. Donald sat alert, frowning. Then lights swept across the ceiling and the car drove into the garage. In a few minutes I heard Dale come into the kitchen and on to the living room where he held out the car keys.

"If it's all right with Maggie," Donald said, "I'd be grateful if you'd drive me home. Something seems to have delayed Philippe. Anyhow I'd rather like a word with you."

"A pleasure," Dale said, "if you'll wait, sir, until I get the car out again."

When the car was at the door, he came to help Donald with his overcoat and give him his crutch. He steered him carefully down the steps. Behind his back the thumb and forefinger of his free hand made a triumphant circle.

182

EIGHTEEN

Next morning I got up before Hazel was awake, before Gerald was apt to be awake either, but I wanted to talk to him at home and not at his office where Terry might be able to overhear.

It was Mrs. Flower who answered the telephone. "It's only seven o'clock, Miss Maggie," she protested, "and Mr. Stephens generally sleeps until eight and has his breakfast at eight-thirty. I hardly like—"

If I asked him to call me back after breakfast, Hazel would be hovering around. "It's really important. But don't alarm him. We're both well and all that."

"If you'll take the responsibility."

It didn't take long to awaken Gerald. "What's up, Maggie?" he asked in his usual calm voice.

While I poured out a rather incoherent story, he listened without interruption. At the end he said, "You've gotten yourself all stirred up, haven't you?"

"Well, thinking that you were being cheated on all sides, I just couldn't bear it, and I know you'd want it stopped."

"Now, I'll tell you what I've picked up—just a minute. Mrs. Flower, I'd like some coffee now, please. In the first

183

place, Sam and I have had a long talk. He told me what he, the government boys, your friend Curtis, and a dog had discovered at my warehouse. I understand my old night watchman is already under arrest. Now we aren't wasting any time. Our government men are in touch with their French counterparts and old man Thibault and his gang are being picked up. At least one source of heroin is being stopped.

"However, we are keeping the story out of the papers and making sure no word of warning gets through from the French end. I still haven't any tangible proof against Terry. Oh, I know she was with her Philippe the night I spent at your house. I saw her with those binoculars you left with me as a joke. Well, hardly a joke, is it, when you have had blind faith in a person for more than five years?"

"She is still working for you?" I was incredulous.

"You mustn't think I have any doubt. I simply want some legal proof. After all, her personal life is no concern of mine, and if she is involved with Philippe, it may have no connection with the smuggling."

"Do you really believe that?"

"No," he admitted, "I don't believe it. Perhaps it is true that everyone has in him a touch of larceny if given the right stimulus."

"And you don't really believe that either. You're trying to find some excuse for her," I accused him.

"Perhaps. But, for God's sake, Maggie, come back here until this thing is solved. You're too close to the scene of action and to two enigmatic figures about whom I'd like to know a lot more."

"Who are they?"

"Dale Curtis and Donald Gregory."

"Donald! But the man is an invalid. And, as you must have seen for yourself, he's a gentle, well-bred, delightful man. He

184

was involuntarily involved only because Terry had to move Philippe in a hurry to the twin house. Donald just happened to be in the market for a quiet place in the country. Last night I told him about the relationship between Terry and Philippe and warned him that he might be in danger because Philippe is a murderer and involved in heroin smuggling."

"Trusting Maggie!"

"That's just what Donald said."

On the whole the call was unsatisfactory. Gerald was insistent that I return at once. I was determined to see the thing out to its finish.

I made coffee and was scrambling eggs when Dale came in. He was obviously taken aback at seeing me and not at all pleased.

"What are you doing up at this hour?"

"I'll put on some more eggs for you," I said.

He nodded, took the cup of coffee I gave him, and went out of the kitchen carrying it. He closed the door behind him and I heard him dialing. He waited a long time and if he spoke, I couldn't hear a word. Then he dialed another number and this time, because I was straining to hear, I caught an indistinguishable murmur. Then his voice rose in an exultant shout.

"Good work! So we've got the bastard."

He was silent again and finally I heard him say clearly, "A child would have known better. To let him slip out of your hands like that. . . . Well, what are you doing?"

When he came back to the kitchen, his face was bleak. He set down the untasted coffee which had grown cold and I poured it out and refilled the cup. I pushed a plate of scrambled eggs toward him. I was dying to ask questions but I managed to keep still. For a moment he shoved the eggs around on his plate, tasted them, and began to eat hungrily. I made more toast and refilled his cup.

185

When he had eaten his fill, he looked across the table and smiled at me. "You'll make a good wife, Maggie. Like the wife of Coriolanus. 'My gracious silence.' "

Breakfast is no time for dalliance, so I kept a firm grip on the situation. "I only waited until you had eaten all you wanted."

He shouted with laughter and some of the fatigue and defeat went out of his face and his head regained its arrogant stance, the big nose like the prow of a ship.

"Okay," he said, turning to make sure the kitchen door was closed, "how do you want it? Good news first or bad news?"

"Good news. It will fortify me for the rest."

"As soon as Philippe had left Gregory here and gone to meet Chris, I went to the twin house where I was met by the government boy who found Prescott's body, and a couple of men from the state police, equipped with cameras, fingerprint material, and a dog trained to scent out dope. A whole detection army."

"Did you find the heroin?"

"It was in the mattress in Philippe's room. Very neat job. Packaged in a dozen different ways and ready to be turned over to the men who sell it to the victims. A hell of a haul. Probably half a million dollars' worth. Apparently Terry brought the stuff up with her every time it was shipped and turned over to her by the night watchman."

He had come to an abrupt halt and I prodded him. "Go on. The suspense is hurting me."

"I hope the rest of it won't."

"Please, Dale!"

"As I say, we took along the usual fingerprint equipment."

"Do I have to prod every word out of you?"

"We found Philippe's prints all over the place and a lot of Terry's—which a man picked up from her telephone in New

186

York—but they weren't where you'd expect to find them. The window you can see from this house is not Philippe's, it is Gregory's."

I stared at him.

"Terry, according to our French friends, is really Thèrese Thibault, Philippe's sister. Her lover is Gregory."

"Oh, poor Donald! How awful for him." Then I gave Dale an accusing look. "You knew it all the time."

"Well, I suspected it. Hazel has a good eye, you know. I spotted at once the resemblance between Philippe and Terry, same shape of nose, same way the ears are set, same skull structure, same coloring. Thick glasses and that wig made a terrific difference."

"So Donald has been used by both brother and sister. And after all he's gone through, too!"

"Well, Maggie, you're a big girl now. If you could rid yourself of this absurd blindness about the charming Donald Gregory—" He waited politely for a retort, but I was silent. "There's one thing that struck me when you gave me your slightly maudlin description of your tenant, and that was the rubber gloves he never removes. I began to think about them."

"I told you he was in an explosion and was badly scarred. You can see the scars on his scalp and the sort of odd shape to his nose. And his stiff leg—"

"I'm beginning to wonder," Dale remarked, "whether you'd be the ideal wife after all. This susceptibility to handsome men, this mindless capitulation to phony charm—"

I picked up a glass of water but he reached across the table to take it out of my hand. "Mustn't throw things. Very bad form. Well, my innocent friend, there are other ways of accounting for scars on the scalp. That is one result of a face-lifting job. A nose can be remodeled. There's a curious lack of expression in Gregory's face, hadn't you noticed?

187

That isn't simply the restraint of a strong, silent man—"

"Oh, shut up!" I said crossly.

"You'd die of curiosity if I did." He was deliberately infuriating. "The thing is that your tenant has had a complete and very efficient job of plastic surgery, what is known as cosmetic surgery, the sort of thing aging actresses go in for, and silly women who want to keep their youth."

"But I told you the man was in an explosion—"

"Don't interrupt the professor until he has concluded the lecture. Suppose a man wanted or needed to alter his appearance so he would not be recognized. A plastic surgeon, if paid enough—and God knows this filthy racket pays enough!— would be happy to oblige."

"You are trying to make me believe Donald is a part of this business?" I asked furiously.

Dale came around the table, lifted me up, sat down and pulled me onto his lap, the long fingers of one hand clamped lightly over my mouth.

"Well, a guy can change his face or his hair or, by contact lenses, the color of his eyes. But he can't change his fingerprints. Hence the surgical rubber gloves. But though he probably wore them all day long to keep from leaving prints, it's unlikely he slept in them or bathed in them. He was careful; I'll say that for him. We found only a couple of fingerprints: one on a tube of toothpaste and one on the edge of the bathroom mirror.

"Well, the lab men did a rush job and the FBI came through this morning. The prints are on record. Donald Gregory is no other than Dustin Gorman, a few years ago a popular college instructor in sociology who met the glamorous Thèrese Thibault, fell for her, hook, line and sinker, and was drawn into the dope racket.

"Not being as experienced or as ruthless and tough as the Thibaults, he was the one to be caught. That was bad luck because he tried to shoot it out and got a bullet in the leg that shattered a kneecap. He spent his year in prison in a hospital bed. Yes, just one year. There are powerful forces behind these dope rings, which bring in millions, tens of millions of dollars a year."

Dale dropped his hand from my mouth and lifted me off his lap. His eyes were sober as he searched my face.

"What's going to become of him?" I asked numbly.

"When I drove him back to his house last night, I could see he was in a state of jitters. He hasn't the tough fiber of his companions. I don't know what you'd said to get him in that state."

"It wasn't I. Hazel came tearing down from the attic to say that there were lights at Donald's house, and a police car. And, of course, Philippe had failed to come for him."

"Dear Hazel! She never fails, does she? Well, I think Gregory intended to question me, but he was too rattled. Of course we'd cleared up before I came back home, working like demons to get the whole thing done because we didn't know how much time we had. I could see the cars going down the hill when I brought the Gremlin around, so I gave them time to disappear. You can see car lights for a long time. That's why I took my time coming in for Gregory.

"Well, we carried out the comedy. I gave him his crutch and was most solicitous about helping him into the house. He switched on the lights, looked around, and shouted for Philippe. When he turned to thank me for the lift, he looked ghastly. Like a dead man."

"And that's the bad news? That Donald is the head of the dope smuggling gang."

"No," Dale said grimly, "the bad news is still to come. Last night, in order to clear the house so we could search it, Chris laid on a meeting with Philippe, indicating that he was willing to pay well to get a supply of heroin for his clients.

189

We'd set it up to have someone follow Chris wherever he went. They met in the village drugstore and didn't come out. After twenty minutes the man following Chris went in—the Daimler was still parked on the street in front. Chris, who has been staying at Luigi's tavern, had come on foot. There were a couple of kids at the soda fountain, a pharmacist behind a counter, a woman clerk just closing up the cosmetics for the night. No trace of the two men.

"There was a back entrance, the woman clerk said, adding coyly that you had to go past the Gents and Ladies to reach it. Most of their supplies were brought in the back way. She remembered Philippe. 'Something about him. Real sexy.' " Dale snorted. "She didn't remember Chris at all. No sign of the men in back, of course. The pharmacist went out and let out a howl when he found his car was gone. He gave the license number. Thumbtacked to the back door was a note. It read:

"No pursuit and complete immunity and you get your man back alive. Otherwise we'll tell you where to find the remains. Our freedom first.

That's the news that hit me just now when I called. I don't for the life of me see how they managed to take Chris off guard. He knew what he was dealing with. He knew the risks."

"What are the police going to do?"

"They aren't going to risk Chris's life, but they aren't going to let Philippe get away with it either. God only knows how they'll handle it. What I can't figure out is how Philippe got onto Chris. His whole approach had been cautious, step by step, leading up to flashing the billfold and dropping hints that he was in the market. I suppose in a dangerous setup like that, they are always on their guard, always suspicious."

190

He looked so defeated I couldn't bear it. "Look, Dale, there must be some way of counterattacking."

"Such as what?"

"Grab Terry. An eye for an eye."

He leaped for the telephone and dialed. When he turned back, his face was blank. "Too late. She left her apartment sometime during the night. They are all clearing out while they can. The racket is fine but the prospect of spending the rest of their lives in prison is not so good, and they've got a murder and kidnaping added to their record now."

"What's the number of Terry's car?" I asked.

Some of the defeat faded from Dale's face. He smiled. "You never give up, do you, darling?" He gave me a bear hug. "They've sent that out to six states, but she'll probably change cars before the police can get moving. It takes time."

The kitchen door opened. "Well, hello, early birds!" Hazel was at her brightest. "Oh, I see you've already had breakfast. No, don't bother to do the dishes, Maggie. You know I am always more than willing to do anything I can to help." She sighed bravely. "You can't imagine all the excitement last night, Dale. Donald's house must have been burglarized. There was a state trooper's car and I don't know what all. I hope everything was all right when he got back."

"Perhaps," Dale suggested, "I had better go over and see."

"Alone?" I could not help that protest.

"I'll have plenty of company," he said cryptically.

"Be sure to tell him—anything we can do—" Hazel said.

Dale's lighthearted grin was back. "I'll tell him," he promised.

NINETEEN

Hazel, as usual, had her transistor radio going as loud as possible so that she would be sure to hear it over the noise of the vacuum. From the second floor, where I was making beds, I could hear the thing blare. Looking across at the twin house, I could see no sign of activity. Dale had taken neither the Gremlin nor the motorcycle, so I assumed he wanted to remain inconspicuous.

What was happening over there? Was Donald under arrest or was he waiting, cornered, for someone to come for him? But if Terry had left her apartment during the night, she must be here by now. Surely the house must be under guard. I stood looking out of the window and folding the red scarf Luigi's wife had lent me.

The vacuum fell with a thud and in a moment Hazel came rushing up the stairs calling, "Maggie! Maggie!"

"What is it?"

"I just heard on the radio that Philippe Thibault has kidnaped a man named Christopher Lamb and left word that he wanted a guarantee of freedom or this man would be put to death. The police have announced that they refuse to make a deal. Surely they won't let that poor man die."

"I don't know."

"Poor Donald. So awful for him. Well, I'd better put away that silver centerpiece. I started to do it last night but I forgot when I noticed all the activity going on over at Donald's." She trotted up the attic stairs.

The phone rang and I went down to answer it as someone walked briskly across the hall. Dale had come back already. But when I reached the first floor, it was not Dale but Donald who stood smiling at me. Donald without his crutch but holding a small revolver in his gloved hand.

"Come along," he said in his pleasant voice. "Sorry I can't give you time to get a coat. No, don't make any noise. I don't want Hazel buzzing around my head. And your friend Curtis has been taken care of." He gestured with the revolver. "I don't want to shoot you if it can be avoided. Move."

"Where?"

He held out my car keys which we kept hanging beside the kitchen door. "Out the back way, please." With the gun prodding my back, I led the way to the garage and got into the car in the passenger's seat.

"No," he said, "you are going to drive. I'm riding in back. At the faintest indication that you are prepared to call for help, you'll get it. Sorry to be so melodramatic, but the cards are all down now but one. You. The government boys apparently are willing to sacrifice their man. I don't think they'd care to sacrifice you. All you have to do is to be a good girl. Put that red scarf on. No one is likely to notice you aren't wearing a coat."

I did so, fumbled with the key, shaking not only with fear but with cold. The car started, rolled out of the garage and turned toward the twin house. Donald was crouching on the floor behind me, the gun steady in his hand. I drove as slowly

193

as I could, but there was no sign of life at the twin house. *Dale had been taken care of.* That was the unspeakable thing, the unbearable thing.

Shock does queer things to people. I was not aware of grief. I was more furiously angry than I had ever been in my life. Someone had deliberately murdered Dale. I was too angry to be afraid and the release of adrenalin or something made me more alert, started my stunned mind working.

"Pick up a little speed now," Donald said, sitting up. "But don't do anything to attract attention."

"Where are you taking me?"

"You have guts, haven't you, Maggie? I'm sorry, you know," and he sounded sincere, "that this had to happen to you. Such a very nice girl. I think, during the past few years, I had forgotten what it was like to meet a girl who was honest and brave and trusting. Too trusting. Poor Maggie! But I'm in too deep now, my dear. If I'm caught, there will be not only the dope charge but I'm an accessory to Prescott's murder and that would be the end of me. I've been in prison and it's hell. I nearly lost a leg."

"But you can walk."

He laughed. "Oh, yes, outside prison I found a better surgeon."

"A plastic surgeon? What did you look like before, Donald? Before you sold out to a cheap woman, a criminal, a destroyer of people? Somewhere there must still be some decency buried in you."

"Don't count on it, my dear. I hate involving you but you're my last resource. And I won't go back to prison. Death would be pleasanter."

"But not your death. Prescott died because he was doing his job. Chris will have to die because he was trying to stop a hideous racket. Dale—"

194

"Dale? Oh, the heroic avenger of his brother-in-law. Stop here, Maggie."

"Here?" I said blankly and then, unbelievingly, I saw that he had indicated the tavern where Dale and I had talked and eaten supper, where the huge and benevolent Luigi had lent me his wife's red scarf which I was now wearing. And Luigi, my heart leaped at the thought, was working with Dale.

There was only one car in the tavern's parking lot, a shabby Ford that must be nearly ten years old.

"Watch your step," Donald said, and he walked close beside me, one hand in his pocket and the gun nudging my side.

There was only one person in the tavern, a woman sitting in one of the booths. Her smoky black hair was parted in the middle and curled softly at shoulder level. She had thrown off a mink coat and her beautiful body was revealed in a cream-colored knit dress. She had long heavily lidded eyes and a ripe mouth crimson with lipstick. She looked up as we entered the tavern and at the same moment Luigi came through the swinging door.

"Your milk punch," he said, and set it down before her with a flourish. He turned to us, indicating a booth, saw the scarf and his eyes widened. I gave him a blank stare and took a quick step toward him. Instantly Donald was beside me. Luigi's mild expression did not change, but his eyes flickered.

Donald prodded me toward the booth. "Well, darling, have you been waiting long?"

"It seemed long," she said in a slow husky voice, but now I knew who she was and stared incredulously. "Terry!"

To my despair Luigi had gone back to the kitchen again. He was my only hope. Then he returned. "What can I get you?"

"Coffee, please," I said.

195

"Sorry," Donald intervened, "I'm afraid we haven't time. If you've finished that milk punch—"

Terry pushed it away, untouched, and I saw the glitter of diamonds on her fingers, a diamond bracelet on her wrist, diamonds in her ears. Probably that was the safest way of investing her money.

I wanted to pull off the head scarf and give it to Luigi. Certainly he had recognized it. But it was wiser perhaps not to let Donald know that I knew the man and the man knew Dale.

When we got outside, Donald tossed my car keys into the snow and Terry slid under the wheel of the old Ford. Donald pushed me into the back seat and told me to sit on the floor, and threw an ancient carriage robe over me, filthy and dusty, but at least it was warm.

Now at last I understood what Donald had meant when he had said he would like to be a purveyor of dreams, that dreams sweetened life and made it more bearable. Heroin that helped a man or a woman or a little child to escape the burden of reality until the need led to total destruction. It was apparent that neither Terry nor Donald sought this particular form of escape for themselves.

Terry drove, as she did everything else, efficiently. Once out of the village she headed north, driving very fast.

"Any word from Philippe?" Donald asked her. There was no reason to hesitate about talking in front of me. Before long it wouldn't matter what I overheard.

"You heard the broadcast? They aren't playing!" A stream of filthy language came pouring from Terry's lips.

"Where is Philippe headed?"

"Canadian border. Jacques has a plane waiting on a private field."

"Damn it to hell!" Donald exploded. "When I think of the money I have cached in a safety deposit box in Hartford."

"Haven't you any traveler's checks?"

"Oh, sure, and a complete identity to go with them, of course, but just the same—all that risk for nothing."

"About two hundred thousand for your share," Terry said dryly. "And me besides."

"How much is Philippe clearing out of this?"

"Half a million, more or less, but he's been sending most of it to our uncle for safekeeping. After all, he took the most risk. He got rid of Prescott. He'll get rid of this snooper."

"How?"

Terry shrugged. "He'll figure something. Said he'd doped the guy and he won't try anything—final—until we're across the border."

"How long do you figure?"

"Before dark with luck and depending on road conditions and weather. If the snow holds off. Philippe got a head start, of course. Changed to a pickup truck as soon as he could find one with the key in it. Some guy going into a hamburg joint. You have any trouble?"

"Friend Curtis came prowling. I heard him at the back door and waited for him, hit him with my crutch."

"Kill him?" Terry could not have been less concerned.

"Cracked his neck. I've never killed anyone. But there was no choice—him or me." He added, as though he could not help himself, "God, I hated it!"

Dale was dead and his murder was being discussed as a thing of no moment except for Donald's burst of self-pity.

"There's a car following us," Terry said quietly. "May mean nothing, but it's been about three car lengths behind for the past ten minutes."

Perhaps Luigi had noticed that something was wrong. But whom could he call? Dale could not answer. Dale would never answer again. All that arrogant stance, that big proud nose, the strong powerful body, the beguiling grin, all was finished. What happened to me didn't seem to matter now. Anyhow a bullet would be quick.

Terry turned fast, so fast the tires screamed and the old car rocked. She turned again, sending me thumping against the back of the front seat; another screaming turn and I rolled back.

When she spoke, her voice was as unhurried as ever. "If anyone was following us I threw him off. Anyhow, I abandoned my car in the Bronx and picked up this one from the driveway of a deserted house marked 'For Rent.' It's unlikely anyone could be on our track, but I don't believe in taking chances."

Donald laughed at that.

"I wish this damned car had a radio. The hunt's on for Philippe and I want to know what's happening."

"I wish," and Donald's pleasant voice sounded unutterably weary, "we could have gone on as we were. No risks. Money pouring in. If only Philippe had had the sense not to kill Prescott. After all, the poor devil really didn't know anything. He just guessed."

"There's no sense in looking back. The real trouble started when Maggie came back and wanted to move out to her house before we could clear things up properly and sidetrack the telephone calls." Terry did not bother to raise her voice. "You'll pay for that, Maggie, my love. Pay and pay and pay."

"No funny stuff," Donald said. "There are other ways."

"She has it coming to her."

"But—"

"Look, darling, let's get one thing clear. I run the show. I always have. And at this moment I've got on me every penny I ever made: diamonds in my bra, in a money belt, in the lining of my coat. Enough to live high the rest of my life. And that's what I mean to do. You can't do that and be soft.

It's Maggie's freedom or mine. Are you going my way or not?"

There was a long silence. "Weakening?" Terry asked mockingly.

"Sometimes I think I hate you," Donald said, "but I can't do without you. You're evil but you're in my blood."

Terry laughed.

Drawn together by a bond that neither one could break, a bond that held as much hatred as love. Like Antony and Cleopatra, flying together as though pulled by magnets, but turning on each other when things went wrong.

We had been riding a long time. I was chilled and cramped and hungry and frightened and heartsick.

At length Terry said, "We've got to stop for fuel. While the tank's being filled, I'll go get some sandwiches and beer and a bottle of vodka. No one would recognize me as Theresa Tilson." She drove up to a filling station and got out. Then unexpectedly the back door opened and cold air bit into my face. "Just in case Donald gets feeling sorry for you—" She pulled up the sleeve of my sweater.

"Terry!" Donald expostulated.

"It's all right," she said impatiently. "Just give her a nice quiet sleep." A needle jabbed inside my elbow.

TWENTY

I tried to shift my position because my legs were cramped and found that I could not move. For a moment I thought I was paralyzed and then I was completely awake. I was aware of the vibrations on the floor of the car, of lying huddled under the filthy carriage robe, chilled to the bone and nauseated. For a few moments I fought an almost losing battle with the nausea and then I pulled the robe away from my face and breathed deeply. Gradually my stomach settled.

I remembered now where I was and what had happened. Donald and Terry had taken me prisoner. Dale was dead and his friend Chris had been kidnaped by Philippe and would be killed after they reached the Canadian border when the three of them would escape by plane for France and freedom.

But they wouldn't, I thought, get away with it. They did not know that the French authorities were watching Terry's uncle. They would be picked up and extradited to the United States for trial on charges of kidnaping and murder and dope smuggling. I wondered if it would help me to tell Terry it would serve no purpose to kill me, that she had no chance of living high for the rest of her life. She might as well let me go.

But perhaps she did have a chance. So far they held the cards. They were free. Dale was dead. Chris would die. I would die.

But to be led meekly to the slaughter like animals waiting to be butchered, without a struggle! There must be something to be done. Hazel must know I'd left the house. But you could never tell what Hazel would do. Luigi? He had recognized me; at least he had recognized his wife's scarf, and he had known Dale well; he had known that Terry had visited Donald's house; he had sheltered Chris. He'd call someone, do something. But who could find me in time? No one would be looking for an old Ford left at a deserted house.

Some instinct of self-preservation, the instinct that keeps the mouse still behind the hole outside which the cat waits, made me lie as quietly as I could. I risked opening my eyes and knew that it must be late, not only because of the darkness but because as we passed through a small town there were only a few lights burning.

Slowly, inch by inch, I raised my head, straining to see. Then I made out a name and saw that we were in Vermont. We must be nearing the border. The sands were running out.

When Donald spoke suddenly, I almost gasped in surprise. The couple in front had not spoken for a long time.

"How do we get across the border?"

"It's tricky. Past an old farm and along a dirt road that will probably be hell to find in the dark. If it hadn't been for the flat tire and the oil leak, we should have been here long ago."

"It would be great to run into a border guard."

"We won't. Philippe has made this trip often. As we get near the border, a helicopter will pick up our lights—there's no one else on the road, thank God—and guide us to the field where the plane will be waiting. Philippe will meet us there."

"I hope you can find the way. Otherwise—"

"God, you're really losing your nerve, aren't you? If you weren't so damned good-looking, I'd have dropped you a long time ago. This is no time for nerves."

"Have you ever suffered from nerves, Terry?"

She laughed. "Nerves! I've never felt so exultant in my life. I've got a fortune on me, Don! Two millions in diamonds. We can go on working if we please, and the trade is just as good abroad, if we keep this side of the Iron Curtain. They don't play over there. Or we can take it easy. Paris, Cairo, Monaco. Barbados is heaven in winter. You can get another face and no one knows mine anyhow. Free! Free! Free!" She flung out a hand and then caught the wheel to steady it as the car swerved on the icy road.

"All you see is a rosy future, isn't it? Leaving behind three bodies. Gerald Stephens is a big man and he knows you are tied up with Philippe. He won't sit back and do nothing. He cares more about that girl we have in back than you've ever cared about anything in your life. Let him have back the girl, unhurt, and we've got it made. Otherwise we are leaving behind burned bridges. The point of no return."

"So let the bridges burn," Terry said. "Look ahead, not behind you."

"In some ways you are a fool, Terry. I tell you that girl is our only chance. Let her go. For God's sake, let her go! You don't need to release her until we're ready to get in the plane. But let her live."

"Shut up!"

"But—"

"I mean shut up. I want to listen."

I ventured to raise my head an inch or two off the floor, away from the vibrations, straining to hear.

"That's the 'copter. I told you so, my faint-hearted friend." Terry switched the lights on and off. We could hear it clearly now; it seemed to be hovering almost directly overhead. Then the sound faded away.

"It's gone."

"It's leading the way." Terry was impatient. "We'll follow it. We're almost there now."

"Are you sure it's the right 'copter?"

"Oh, for God's sake, what else? If you can't keep still, at least try to make sense. I have all I can do to keep this car on the road. I'll bet the tires are worn smooth."

But, perhaps, I thought—because hope dies hard, or perhaps it never dies—Luigi, sleepy-looking Luigi, who had been a friend of Prescott's and had his own personal score to settle, had checked on the license of the Ford and had reported it. Someone, somewhere, might be looking for me. And with hope beginning to stir I tensed, prepared to fight. I wasn't going to be eliminated without a struggle. And somehow I believed now that my only real danger was Terry. I did not think Donald could bring himself to shoot me.

"We're nearly there," Terry said. "See, the 'copter is coming down. This must be the private flying field." She gave a little exclamation of triumph. "See the lights over there? High up? That's the plane warming up. Philippe must have ditched the pickup truck by now."

"And his hostage?"

"What do you think? Philippe will hardly want a fourth at bridge on this flight."

"And Maggie?"

"Leave her to me."

"No, I can't do it, Terry. God knows I've been accessory to enough. I killed Curtis in self-defense, but the girl—no! I'm the one who's had to take it in the past. I'm the one who was shot, the one who was imprisoned, the one who had to

203

go through months of surgery. And every time you and Philippe came off unscathed."

"*Tais toi!*"

"Terry," and there was more feeling in Donald's voice than I would have believed possible, "let the girl go."

"Or else?" she mocked him.

"Don't drive me too far!"

She laughed at that. "You'll go where I tell you, Don. I know just how far you're capable of balking, and just where your nerves break."

She brought the car to a jolting halt and she blinked the lights. Both doors slammed as she and Donald got out. Then the back door opened.

"Well," Terry said, "so you're awake. Little Bright Eyes!"

Painfully I started to get up from the crouching position in which I had lain for hours.

"No," Terry said, "just stay where you are. You might as well be comfortable. You're going to be there a long, long time."

"Terry," Donald said, "what are you going to do?" He was standing beside her, his collar turned up around his ears, wearing a heavy muffler and a cap with earflaps. The latter must have been purchased somewhere along the way, as I was sure he had not worn them when we started out. He looked down at me, his handsome face drawn, and I stared back, holding his eyes, until they shifted away from me.

Terry's hand darted out, reached inside his coat pocket and brought out the revolver.

"No! For God's sake, no!"

"Oh, turn away if you don't like it," she said in a tone of weary disgust.

And Donald, unbelievably, turned his back and covered his ears with his hands, like a child.

"Help!" I shouted. "Help!" But I was shouting to nobody,

nowhere. Just making an involuntary appeal. And then, humiliatingly, I was crying, "Please, please, please."

Feet were pounding toward us and Terry turned in relief. "Philippe! Here, you do this. I've never shot anyone." Then she gave a thin, shrill scream.

"It's about the only thing you haven't done, isn't it?" As Terry gave another scream, this time of pain rather than terror, the voice said, "I'm sorry to hurt you, but I'll really have to have that gun, you know. People like you shouldn't be allowed to play with dangerous toys." It was a pleasant voice with a Harvard accent, but it wasn't Dale's. Whoever he was, he was no friend to Terry.

"She's all yours," he called, and two men emerged from behind him, vague figures moving on the dimly lighted flying field.

"Who are you?" Terry demanded. "Where is Philippe?"

"Well, in a way I'm the smile on the face of the tiger. He figured he had put me out with that drink he offered me and I dumped it and played along until we got out of town and then I—persuaded him to pour out his little heart to me."

"Where is he?"

"Trussed up in the back of that pickup truck. Or—" He turned and looked toward a truck where some sort of activity was going on. "Well, at the moment he is being given a warm welcome by the Canadian police. But, if my guess is any good, there will be some authorities from the other side of the border along to take him back. Okay," he called to the two men behind him, "these are all yours. Take them along. This is Thérèse Thibault, wanted on smuggling heroin and implication in the murder of a man named Prescott. Her stooge here is Dustin Gorman, *alias* Donald Gregory, once a popular young college instructor, more recently a convict who made the mistake of shooting a cop when he was caught passing heroin. Only got a year that time because he had

205

influence behind him. Now he's going to have a nice long rest."

Terry shook off impatiently the hand that had closed over her arm. "I don't know how much you want, but you'll find me reasonable. A hundred thousand to let my brother and me make that plane."

"Lady, it would be worth that much to me just to see you jugged for life, as I sincerely hope you will be."

I could see his face now. The man who had taken Terry's arm had been just behind Chris.

"Who are you?" Terry demanded.

Chris looked at her. "It doesn't matter who I am. Meet my friends from the Canadian police."

Chris brushed Terry aside and leaned into the back of the car to drag me out. I was so numb I couldn't stand. There were, I saw now, a number of men milling around and one of them came quickly to help steady me.

"How badly are you hurt?" Chris asked.

"Just cold and stiff and a little sick from the shot she gave me and," I remembered, "hungry."

Chris picked me up in his arms. "We'll get you indoors first, and get you warm and fed." The man beside him stripped off his overcoat and put it around me.

"Now that's a good idea."

Donald stood, shoulders slumping, staring at his feet. He looked up. "Maggie, I did try to save you."

I began to laugh and when I started, I found I could not stop. "He turned away and c-covered his ears."

Chris shook me. "Cut that out," he said sternly. "This is no time for hysterics, though I admit you have them coming to you."

I took a long shuddering breath and said nothing until we were inside a small shack at one side of the private flying field. There was a pot-bellied stove in the middle of the room

206

and the smell of coffee. Chris set me down but I still couldn't stand. My legs were like cooked spaghetti. He pushed me gently into a chair, went to bring me a cup of scalding coffee, and steadied my hand while I drank.

"Nothing to eat but doughnuts," he said apologetically, "but we'll have you back on your native shores as soon as the Canadian authorities get through."

"How did you find me? I don't understand any of this."

Chris turned to the tall man who had given me his overcoat. He was probably in his middle forties, with an ordinary sort of face and rimless glasses. He looked more like a college professor before they went beatnik than the man who had organized the search for the smuggling band and had headed the pursuit. In the movies these things are much more dramatic.

"Just a question of teamwork, Miss Barclay," he said casually. "Of course we owe a lot to Dale Curtis. He's the one who finally pinpointed your house as the distribution center for the heroin. After that, it was just a matter of routine. We discovered, again through Curtis, where the stuff was coming from and how the Stephens importing firm was being used. So when you arrived on the scene and we learned that Prescott had disappeared, we put a man on the job of looking for the body, which he found on your land, after you had practically fallen into the grave. By that time it was apparent that you were being driven away and the house had strange uses, people who didn't show except for the occasional carelessness of revealing lights.

"There was one odd character, the man Philippe Thibault, who seemed to have no domicile but kept appearing around the village until he recently landed a job with Donald Gregory, who had rented the twin house. It wasn't until Curtis arranged with his friend Chris here to keep Philippe busy for an evening that Curtis and the government men and the state

207

police searched the twin house and found this guy's finger-prints."

Donald looked up at that. "Dale Curtis again." His lips curved in an expression of satisfaction. At least he had evened his score with Dale.

Chris broke in then. "This I must have the pleasure of saying myself, sir. Tonight you tried to murder Dale, left him for dead with a broken neck. But we had a guy watching; he saw you force Miss Barclay into her own car. And the lame Mr. Gregory was walking just fine! We've had word that Dale was only knocked out. He's on his way here now. Couldn't hold him back."

He turned to Terry. "You've got quite an army to welcome you, Miss Thibault: American government men, state police, Canadian police. Mr. Stephens got onto the state police as soon as he heard of Miss Barclay's abduction. He was tele-phoning her when the thing happened and got the story from the other Miss Barclay. Of course the Connecticut State Police have no jurisdiction here but our neighbors are willing to let them sit in on the finale. They don't care for smugglers either, or the effects of heroin, or murder, or kidnaping."

Terry spoke for the first time since she had learned that her brother was under arrest. "How the hell did you trace us?"

"We never lost sight of you. When the tavernkeeper, Luigi, saw Miss Barclay in his wife's scarf and no coat and looking scared to death, he got the setup at once. He was an old friend of Prescott's; they used to play checkers together. He got the number of the pickup truck and painted the top with fluorescent paint. You've been escorted all the way."

"The 'copter?"

"Property of Uncle Sam. And, in case you still think you could make it to France, the plane waiting over there is a private job that is going to take you back where you came from. The pilot of the one you hired is busy doing some fast talking. And your dear old uncle, who taught you and your brother your delightful trade, is in jail in Marseilles, and what the authorities are finding out at that end makes their hair curl."

"Well," said the tall, quiet man from the government, "if all the paper work is done and the extradition is clear, let's get the show on the road."

And then, moving like a rattlesnake coiled to strike, Donald lunged for the gun Chris still held carelessly in his left hand. Before anyone could stop him, he raised it to his handsome head and pulled the trigger.

TWENTY-ONE

The plane was warm enough so that I could return the nice Treasury man's coat to him. In the woman's room I had done what I could to repair the damage, but I looked like a wreck. One side of my face was discolored from being pressed against the floor of the car. My hair had tumbled down and my arms were too sore and cramped even to attempt to braid it, though I knew how darned conspicuous it was. My only beauty really. Half a dozen times I'd been given offers to model for shampoos. To me it had always been a nuisance and I vowed that the first thing I'd do when I got home was to cut it off.

I said this to Chris, who was in the window seat watching the activity below. There had been a long delay after Donald's suicide and at length his body, covered by a blanket, was slid into the luggage compartment of the plane. I hadn't watched that.

Terry and Philippe, both handcuffed, were at the back of the plane, each in a middle seat with a man on either side of them.

There seemed to be a lot of people, but who they were and what they were doing did not seem to matter to me. All I wanted was to go home and forget it, as though I could.

At my comment about cutting my hair Chris turned to smile at me. "You must be coming out of it. When a woman starts thinking about powdering her nose and fixing her hair, she's okay."

"That's what you think," I retorted, aware that every muscle in my body hurt when I moved. Nevertheless I was in tearing spirits. I understood how Terry had felt when she had cried exultantly, "Free! Free! Free!" Well, she'd never be free again. How often would she think of her diamonds, knowing bitterly that they would do her no good. Do no one any good. I wondered if she would think of Donald with the same regret. Probably not.

But Dale was alive. Knowing that, I couldn't even be sorry for poor, weak, futile Donald, who had thrown away so much. I couldn't be sorry at all. I was in a rush to get home, to find Dale, to tell him—

"What are we waiting for?" I asked.

"A couple more passengers."

"It seemed to me that every department of both governments and the police were here."

"A satisfactory operation on the whole."

"Who else is coming?"

"A special charter flight from home. Two guys who—oh, oh, there they are." I peered out and saw blinking roof lights, car doors slammed, and then men were running toward the plane.

I'd had about all I could take and suddenly I found my hand gripping Chris's sleeve.

"Okay," he said gently. "Okay. All's well."

And then two men were coming down the aisle. One was truly a horrible sight, face cut and streaked with blood, head wrapped in a turban that made him look like a Sikh. Behind him came Gerald Stephens.

211

"Where's my girl?" Dale roared. "What have you done with my girl?" And then he was in the seat beside me and had taken me in a crushing hold. I could feel his heart thudding. I put my arms around his neck and buried my face on his torn and blood-soaked shirt, and howled.

He patted me awkwardly on the back, letting me have my cry out. Then he held me back, looked at me and shook his head. He groped in his torn pocket. "Anyone got a clean handkerchief?"

He wiped the blood from his shirt off my cheek, held me back to see whether I was clean, said, "That's better," and kissed me. It was quite a kiss.

I didn't even notice when the plane took off. I was contented to rest quietly in Dale's arms, with my head on his shoulder. Now and then I sniffled, and I was shaken by a sob, but there was no unhappiness in me. No more fear. Nothing but this feeling of belonging.

Over my head Dale and Chris were talking quickly, while each described what had happened to him and how the Treasury man, whose name was Smith, had built, step by step, a net out of which the Thibaults could not escape and had kept an eye on us all the time.

A FASTEN SEAT BELTS sign flashed on and I stirred at last, released myself from Dale's comforting arms. "Dale, I don't want to go back to that house."

"You don't need to."

"But Hazel—all alone, and nobody even in the next house—"

"For which we devoutly thank God!"

"Amen. But just the same—"

From across the aisle Gerald, who had been watching us with a curious expression, said, "I was just telephoning when that fellow took you away and Hazel saw the whole thing. I got busy. Then word came in about your—friend Dale

212

being knocked up and I arranged to have him brought to meet my chartered plane. I thought you'd need him." He forestalled any comment I might have made. "Sam went up to get Hazel and brought her down. She'll be at the house now, but I thought perhaps you'd rather not cope with Hazel right now. Dale—"

"Why," I said in surprise, "we're at La Guardia. We're in New York."

"The Thibaults will have a lot of questions to answer there and then Philippe will probably have to return to Connecticut to face a murder charge."

As the plane rolled to a halt, Dale stepped back and let Gerald take my arm and guide my still unsteady steps off the plane. "Forgive me, my dear," he said, his voice low. "You remember King Lear, 'Just a foolish fond old man.' We'll both forget it. Anyhow I'm going to be busy, making sure no more skulduggery goes on in my warehouse. Thank God, they've got my watchman dead to rights and Sam wants to take on the job though it's a lot tougher than just driving for me. But I guess it's best to let people follow their own bent. Follow their heart's desire. And that's the last bit of sentiment you'll ever hear from me."

"But, Gerald, you're right about Hazel. I couldn't face her questions tonight—this morning, whenever it is. And how can I go to a hotel looking like that?"

"No self-respecting hotel would let you in, my sweet," Dale commented. "Me either for that matter. I'm taking you to my sister. She's prepared to expect the worst, so it won't be the shock to her it would be to anyone else, getting a first look at my love."

I laughed. "Sure she won't mind?"

"What can the poor girl do? She has to get used to you sooner or later. Probably sooner. No use dragging these things out. Say, next week? When we both look less as

213

though it had taken a shotgun to force us into holy matrimony."

To my relief Gerald gave a laugh of genuine amusement. "It sounds as though you had met your match, Maggie."

"Oh, God!" Dale exclaimed. "Reporters. Photographers. The works. We should have expected it. Well, let's make it as fast as we can. And that reminds me, Chris, when we have escaped those ghouls, you're going with us to Isabelle's."

Chris's face lighted up.

"Strike while the iron is hot, man! Here is your chance to be a hero. What Isabelle needs isn't sympathy; it's a strong guy to lean on. Bill was swell, but he did all the leaning. If you can't take it from there, I give you up."

Dale was on one side of me, Gerald on the other, forming a kind of bodyguard. "All right, boys and girls, let's make it fast," Dale said to the waiting men and women from the media. He turned to the Treasury man. "Will you do the talking, sir? What are we waiting for?"

Along the passage in front of us came Philippe, handcuffed, a man on either side. Cameramen rushed forward, took pictures, men in the background shouted questions. Philippe slouched by without a word.

Next came Terry, also handcuffed, also escorted. But her head was high, her lovely soft hair curled around her face, the lipsticked mouth smiled, the long heavy-lidded eyes looked straight at the camera. Terry was going to be her own best defense. Whether it was her awareness of the diamonds or her iron will, she had not given up the fight.

Then it was our turn. Mr. Smith stepped in front of us to make a brief statement:

"As you are doubtless aware, we have succeeded in rounding up a large and flourishing smuggling operation, bringing vast quantities of heroin from France. The entire organization on both sides of the water have been picked up." Smith

214

raised his hand to stop a barrage of questions. "As you can see, the young couple behind me have suffered a terrible experience at the hands of the smugglers. They are being taken now to a place where they will receive the care they need. As soon as they are in a condition to talk, I am sure they will answer your questions freely. This is not the time. Thank you. Good night."

He moved on at an unhurried pace and the men from the press and television stepped back, staring at Dale with his bloodstained clothes and battered face and the great turban, and at me with my bruised face, staggering walk, and the hair that hung around me like a cloud. No one asked a question. I think they realized we were beyond it. But they took pictures.

Sam worked his way through the crowd, caught Gerald's eye, and forced a path for us to the car. He did not even change expression when he looked at Dale and me.

"Home, sir?"

"Yes, drop me first. Where does your sister live, Dale?"

"East Seventy-fourth Street, just off Fifth."

"I asked Miss Barclay to pack Miss Maggie's things," Sam said, addressing no one in particular. "I didn't think she'd want to go back."

"Oh, thank you, Sam."

"I'll put them in the car for you, miss, as soon as Mr. Stephens gets home. He's lost a lot of sleep lately."

"Give us Sam for a wedding present," Dale begged.

"I know when I'm well suited," Sam replied.